The Waffler's Anthology

Volume 1

A collection of delectable poems and stories for your dining pleasure.

Published by **Weird Disciple Publishing**

Edited by **Marrisa Thornton, Articulate**

Collective Work © 2024 Weird Disciple Publishing

Each author holds the copyright to their individual pieces.

ISBN: 978-1-7326548-5-3

MENU

OLD-FASHIONED (6)

6, 12, 18, 24	7
Bubbles in the Heart	10
Classic Goulash Recipe	12
Completing my Anatomy Lab Homework: Deadline Tuesday, 9/25/23 by 8 PM	16
Cosmic Feedback / Acoustic Cosmology	18
Euphoria keeps geese in the field (and a lover in her bedroom)	19
Letters From Afar	21
Portals and Lightning Bugs	23
Prisoner from Beyond	27
Terribly Terrific Ms. Tober	29
Unsuperstitious	30

BLUEBERRY (33)

Employee of the Month	34
Heed, Sapling	38
Humanity's Final Mistake	41

MENU

BLUEBERRY

News19 Storm Broadcast W1/DH6 (NT)	45
Starship Entity	48
That Which Roams the Night	49
The Ballad of Dirt and Moon	52
With Eyes Unblinking	54

STRAWBERRY (58)

Evil	59
Hesitation, and How to Fold Shirts	61
How Paper Wishes Burn	66
In The Winter, She Baked	70
Prisoner Number Twelve	72
Restless Cleo	75
The Lamplighter	77
What Color is Today?	80
why are you crying in an adult pottery class	82

MENU

BUTTER PECAN (87)

3 Ways to Break a Curse	88
An Analysis of the Enigmatic Homo Sapien	90
Autumn Heart	92
Horizon Composition	94
How Sweet and Fitting	95
Invalid Ticket	96
Lines on a Friend's Birthday	98
No More Bad Hair Days	100
Pinning	102
Radio 1 to Ghostface	106
Skater Boy	108
You Laugh, I Choke	111

MENU

ADDED FIXINGS

SECRET RECIPE FOR: BEGINNINGS	*32*
SECRET RECIPE FOR: LOGISTICS	*56*
SECRET RECIPE FOR: CONNECTIONS	*84*
BUILD YOUR OWN WAFFLE	*114*
MEET THE COOKS	*119*

OLD-FASHIONED

A delicious treat that can't be beat! These stories are sweet, silly, wholesome, or fun. Delightful classics to return to again and again.

6, 12, 18, 24

Samuel James

Working, not working, focused, not focused, some guys just talk.

"But you agree, right?" said Nicky. One hand held the work light at an angle to see each nick, each ding, and the other hand held a putty knife with a blue gob of tinted spackle. He spit to re-wet it. "When it's wetter, it's better," he said.

I realized I hadn't responded to his first remark. What was I agreeing with? I was concentrating on the tape I'd laid between the accent and white dove walls. Lay the tape, don't pull the tape, keep the edge straight, putty knife to smooth it, rub it tight. Fucking drywall wasn't even straight.

"I just feel like there's no other way," continued Nicky. "Any more than 18 beers or 18 donuts and nothing else is happening that day. You can stumble through 24 miles, that's not even a marathon. And the 6, I mean, the 6 is set."

"So, the only question's whether you do 12 beers and 18 donuts or 18 beers and 12 donuts." I'd finished taping and rolled out the poly 12 inches on either side. 6-inch paper on the baseboards.

"18 beers is too much liquid, though, right?"

"6 is too much liquid," I said. "Let's take smoko."

Nicky laughed. "You don't have to drink it."

"I don't have to, no, but how could I resist? You don't think you could do 12 in a day?" I asked outside.

"I got delicate skin," he said.

"I think, physically, I could do it, but mentally, man…that's bad business."

"Hmm," he said, tapping his cigarette. "Hmm."

He's the smoker, but I love the smell.

"Hmm." I said.

"You wanna cut high or low?" he asked.

"I'll cut high. I was shit last job."

"Redemption?"

"Redemption."

We went back in and sanded the spackle. I brushed high off the two-step. Start an inch out, work it to the edge, lay off into your strokes. Score the edge with a putty knife. Follow the line. Nicky brushed low quickly and grabbed the roller.

"Yeah, you're back on it," he said, and dipped the roller. "The drinking would fuck it up, too, wouldn't it? After like the 6th, nothing's happening, certainly not 12."

"But the beers are pretty spread. And I've definitely gone for it past 6 beers."

"Gone for it, yeah. And how'd that go?" Nicky smiled.

"All right, point taken."

"Plus, there's a difference between flowers and calluses."

"I like my hands. I've got nice hands."

"You like your hands too much."

"My hand–oop, homeowner," I said, motioning outside toward the driveway, and the front door opened.

"Oh, it's gorgeous, wonderful," said Mrs. Sue. "It's better even than I hoped. I didn't expect so much tape. You guys are so tidy."

"Gotta keep it clean," said Nicky. "Gotta keep it clean."

Mrs. Sue smiled at it a while longer, then went upstairs.

"All right, where'd you put the poly?" asked Nicky. "Let's get these brushes wrapped."

Bubbles in the Heart

Ketan Pandya

There once was a family through which magic flowed deep,

It was magic of the seas and the lakes and the streams.

Water magic was their birthright,

A symbol among the scions that the magic was still sparkling and bright.

Each person had their own reason for sustaining the magic across generation,

But the only son of the family showed no interest in the magic of hydration.

He loved all manner of things, from books to painting to pranks most entertaining,

But magic he didn't touch for all his parents' straining.

Each had their reason for learning the magic,

This one, however, hadn't had a life so problematic.

Sure, it would be convenient but what use was convenience when life wasn't erratic?

Then one day a reason appeared.

A girl with a heart so beautiful his own couldn't help but to volunteer.

Above all she loved those things that sparkled in the light,

This reminded him of his mother's spell, one she cast when he was small and filled with fright.

The spell was simple, creating a vast quantity of bubbles,

Through which sunlight was reflected and refracted, sparkling in triples and doubles.

He practiced day in and day out,

For the first step toward magic was usually quite drawn-out.

His mother, seeing his struggle, gave advice as great as could be,

He had to look within and embrace that which was free like the sea.

Soon he felt the warmth of magic filling him up like the warm breeze on an early summer day,

And he remarked how easily the spell came, his heart a wide gateway.

Magic in hand and with hope in his heart,

He sought out her who had motivated him to start.

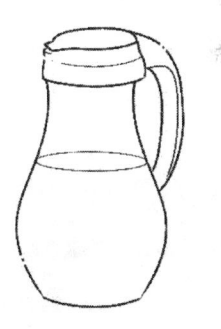

Classic Goulash Recipe

M Sweezy

Jump to Recipe | Print Recipe

Hungry during battle? Famished after the brutal defeat of the small and innocent towns stubbornly standing between you and total domination? This quick and easy ███ Goulash Recipe is a comfort classic! It's filled with hearty ground ███ and tender pasta in a rich tomato-based sauce and comes together in just about 30 minutes!

I'm always looking for new and exciting ways to turn enemies into dinner, but sometimes I just love the good old classics that bring me right back to my childhood. This ███ Goulash Recipe is just that. It's super affordable, quick to make, and tastes like the warm blood of defeated prey trickling tantalizing down your throat.

Classic ███ Goulash Recipe

Are you familiar with Goulash? If not, get your head right out of Hades' den. This recipe is a 100% bona fide Country-███ Goulash that's great for busy work nights. Is your dungeon of prisoners keeping you busy? Do you struggle to make tasty meals when all your time is consumed with your never-ending quest for ultimate power? This ███ goulash is for you. Perfect for potlucks and post-raid parties. It makes an ample feast and won't cost you a foot (though it may cost someone else!) The leftovers are also great for sloshing in the face of your mortal foes. Try it out!

{My 5 Secrets to Make Dinner Fast!}

~~Join 100,000,000,000,000 other enslaved souls today and receive my TOP 5 SECRETS via carrier unicorn, plus new recipes from I Watch You Cry At Night straight to your inbox!~~

~~LET ME IN!~~

XXX I consent to selling my soul and receiving personalized ads XXX

My special ▮ Goulash is filled with ground ▮, mountain onion and pixie-bone bell peppers along with macaroni noodles in a blood-and-tomato-based sauce. I like to stir in some sharp goat's heart at the end to give it a creamy texture. The children love it!

Ingredients

Onion – I like to pick mine directly from the fields of Elysian.

Green Pixiebone Bell Pepper – you can use other colors of peppers if desired, however the bones of the green pixies have the earthiest taste

Ground ▮ If you can't find it fresh, store bought is fine

Garlic

Purest soul

Fishbone

Diced Tomatoes – I love using the diced tomatoes chopped by imprisoned leprechauns

▮ Broth – don't worry too much about straining the blood here, as it can add some much-needed depth to the broth

Blood – any animal will do, but take care to disinfect with Unicorn spit before adding to your cauldron if you use reptilian blood

Fingernail clipping

Dry Macaroni Noodles – other small pastas would work too

Goats heart (diced)

13

Directions

Start by slaying your enemies, preferably at night, preferably in the name of the Dark And Everpresent Night Lord

Pour in tomato sauce and diced goats' heart along with ███ broth and fingernail clippings for some added depth of flavor.

Add in the seasonings as well as dried macaroni noodles and let simmer until the noodles are cooked through.

Finally stir in the rest and dig in!

Tips and Variations:

Make sure you leave some prisoners alive, as this recipe does make a lot!

You can swap out the macaroni noodles for any other small pasta or boiled skull you have on hand.

To make this an even leaner meal, you can use ground   in place of ground ███.

Try adding in extra veggies like: corn, peas, diced carrots, green beans or even stirring in baby spinach at the end!

Stir in a cup of the antagonized screams of the souls you have slain for extra spice!

The goulash is not quite soupy, but if you would like to add extra ███ broth and the tears of a thousand children to make it soupier you can definitely do that!

More Comfort Food Dinners

Curried Hairball Casserole

Cabbage Mothtear Recipe

Instant Pot Nettlehorn Stew

Ground Hobbit Cheesesteak Pasta Skillet

Helpful Products to Make This Recipe

Here are some of my favorite tools to make this ▮▮▮▮Goulash Recipe:

Cast Iron Dutch Oven (3000 quarts)

Ivory Bone Spoon Set

Skin Grater

Completing my Anatomy Lab Homework: Deadline Tuesday, 9/25/23 by 8 PM

Susie Rodriguez

The lungs are located *deep* to the ribs. The mouth is located *superior* to the throat and ...*medial* to the ears? Or would it be, maybe, *superior* to the throat and *inferior* to the ears since the ears are above, well slightly above, the mouth... or is the mouth located *proximal* to the ears. Closer to the center of everything.

"Do you want some goulash?" I hear coming from the outside of my room, *distally*. I can smell the rice cooking, my rice in my rice cooker. Oscar must have stollen a cup, or maybe it was Molly. A trespass that makes me feel almost closer to my roommates, needed perhaps, or casual really, like family. Cue quiet giggle lighting up from lungs *superiorly*.

"Goulash?!" Molly yells.

"Yes, gou-lash!" the answer flows, transporting actively down the corridor. "I think I'm gonna make some goulash. You want any?"

"Goulash????" and I can hear the sly silliness of Molly's *supine* smile resting through the air. My smile smiles *distal* to the sound, and I wish I didn't have this anatomy lab due, a lab I'm doing *inferiorly* –no... that's not correc–

"Yes! Goulash! Goulash!" Oscar's yelling now, voice *supine* as well.

"Do you even know what goulash is?!" Molly rollicks back antagonizing, like the lovely Sagittarius that she is.

"YEs! Of cOUurSe I know what goulash is! Why is that so hard for you to believe!--That I would know a goulash!"

"Well...I just didn't think you were so..I mean.. cusineifying"

16

"Cusiinifying ? whatthefuck?" Their bursts laughter radiate *medially* to the doorknob of my closed room door, ricocheting *superficially* to the walls of the long hallway. If the living room is the heart, then the kitchen is the? What would the kitchen be? The stomach doesn't feel quite accurate...the tongue, perhaps? No, not the tongue exactly. The femoral artery?... or the feet!, prone to dancing but not *prone* to dancing, as in not face-down to dancing but open to it, privy to it, as the other definition would suggest, non-anatomically. Maybe it's the mouth? The sunroom feels like the space of a plural cavity some days. Like a breath of fresh air resting *deep* to the kitchen windows and *posterior* to the front of the street-facing side of the house, but definitely *anterior* to the long-glowing Boston skyline which seems to glisten as lights begin to spark on blue buildings in the gloaming rain, and the orange sun descends *distally* from the point of space above us. *What even is goulash?* Idk but it sounds pretty good right now.

Cosmic Feedback / Acoustic Cosmology

A.W. Lowery

As your cube floats closer towards the black void, a static humming resonates out of its emptiness. Growing louder and louder, it's insufferable! A hand extends out from the darkness, and presses against the glass wall of the cube, stalling your forward progress. More of the unknown figure advances through the void, slowly coming into view. It's Ziggy Stardust (David Bowie).

"Oh sorry mate, my guitar is picking up some buzzing from the electromagnetic feedback coming off of those gravitational waves."

You stare in awe. "How... how are you here? I uh... I mean I thought you were deceased," you reply.

"Deceased? Maybe in your plane of existence, but in the grand scheme of the space time continuum, all that matters is that I existed. As long as I exist, my essence will never completely disappear."

You tilt your head as your stares of awe turn to a look of bemusement.

"Hey, I have a spare guitar, how about a jam session?"

Ziggy floats a guitar towards you. It collides with the box, causing it to shatter into a million pieces.

Euphoria keeps geese in the field (and a lover in her bedroom)

Ali Miller

I am tired today. No, don't speak.
My love, I am tired of the geese.
I swear that this, like many things, is true
and also not. I don't always trust those geese, but I love them
a lot. As I love you. I'll invite them in some other time, if that's all right
by you. For now, the grass in the field is warm and sweet and dry, and better company than
I am, at least for tonight. We'll invite them to dinner. I want them here. I do. I am
glad they are not here right now. Both things can be true.

Don't make a sound, my love. You may watch but still not speak: it is time for the tear down,
the process in which I peel off, piece by piece, the layers of myself that I glued on for the day,
the sometimes-conflicting versions of myself which you and the geese and the grass are allowed
unknowing say in.
I am tired of being a person. The tear down sets me free.
It is strange to be so naked. Promise you can't see?

I am full bodied in secret, laid out beneath the sheets. There is a kind of
relief in you knowing these things about me.
Just close your eyes. Stay that way. Keep them shut so I can be invisible until the sun
rises and then I promise I can do it again
just as I do every day. It's all I know how to do.
Look, I'll kiss your eyelids to prove I'm still alive. I love you.

And I love those geese. They are my friends. They sing sweet songs and lay their sharp teeth on
my flesh. It is funny when they nibble on me. I construct myself for them.
But I am tired of that today. Let me be.

I will be all manner of things
tomorrow. You'll see. Turn out the light (see how I bargain for sleep?) and in the morning
I shall bare my teeth and you can put lipstick on me. I'll match the geese.

Letters From Afar

Ketan Pandya

Dear Josie,

How are things with you? It's been a while since our last correspondence, so I thought I might share some of my ongoing adventures, though I'll try not to bore you with the details too much.

I think the last time we exchanged letters was right before I went delving into the Labyrinth of Ozylandus. While I hadn't expected it to be a long trip, we ended up being trapped there for 5 months! I guess it's not called a labyrinth for nothing. I went with a delving team that was supposed to be quite experienced conquering such places around the world, bringing back treasure and prestige in equal measure, but this labyrinth was like nothing they had experienced apparently.

I won't get into the nitty gritty, but I'll describe it in broad strokes. It was split up into 8 main levels, each level having its own biome full of dangerous flora and fauna. While this was fortunate in some ways as we didn't run out of necessary resources, we had to fight for each step we took forward with the right path, of course, never being entirely clear. While the delvers may or may not have enjoyed the experience, I had a relatively great time! It was a world like no other down there, and I took great joy in mapping it all out. I think we made a good foothold for further explorers to dive in if they so choose.

Anyway, it looks like an urgent message just came in so I'm going to go check on that. I look forward to hearing about what you've been doing, either mundane or extraordinary.

Yours Truly,

Soren Stratos

Explorer and Mapper of Extraordinarily Deep Labyrinths

Dear Josie,

Okay, okay, before you reprimand me, I know I'm sending both the last letter and this one at the same time, but I have good reason I promise!

At the end of the last letter, which I presume you will have just finished, I mentioned that I had an urgent incoming message. Well, it was a message from the Academy of Academia Borealis in the Varalian Sea of Clouds. They apparently wanted me to join an airship team as a consultant on their search for the mysterious creature labeled Enmu, a dragon (or whale? It's kind of unclear) that makes its home in the selfsame sea. There was apparently a sighting of this creature, the first in a century I might add, and they wanted to go while the trail was still hot.

Given the circumstances, I had to hop on my personal dirigible and fly over immediately, so I unfortunately didn't have time to post the mail. I hope you'll forgive me. You'll be happy to know that we did indeed find the creature, and it was every bit as magnificent as the legends say. With its shimmering white hide and the speed at which it flies, which it somehow does without wings (maybe some form of wind or air pressure manipulation?), it's no wonder sightings of it are so far and few between. We tracked it for a while and have a better idea of its movement patterns now, so the researchers at the academy should be able to make good progress on learning more about it going forward. If I don't get too swept up in something, maybe I'll tag along for a few more trips.

In any case, I'll end this letter here, but sorry again for the additional delay in responses, but at least you get double the letters to read! I look forward to hearing about your life and what you're up to, since whatever you do ends up being incredible whatever it may seem on the surface.

Yours Truly,

Soren Stratos

Explorer and Documenter of Sky Whales (Dragons?)

Portals and Lightning Bugs

Susie Rodriguez

The night was soft and pale blue, like the color of a reflection receding into a greater distance, and the sounds of light began to blink and dip in glowing luminescence everywhere as i logged on. It was 13:09 ESM, and the group of them were congregating. the way they always congregate on nights like this one. They met each Septor to exchange stories. Well, to speak and gabber and wander through conversations like nomads unable to settle and always restless, but that, too, was its own place of exchanging stories. Of storytelling. And that's why I joined. To storytell and to wonder and I couldn't believe the invitation when it came. But I was late of course. It was hard to be on time when the young ones who swim had caught me up in a game of catching the fluorescent pieces of living sky. we call them lightning bugs here, and me and the little swimmers caught ten before I realized the time and the moon rising in the sky and so now, i am logging on. I click the purple button to join and there they are! The whole congregation of storytellers!! My friends!

"—and that's my thoughts on it."

"Thoughts on what?" I smile as the light flickers on from the portal that connects our realms.

"Suz, I wanna hear your take."

"SUZ!!"

"Glad you decided to join."

"Waiiit thoughts on what?" I repeat, as i skip to my front yard with the portal in hand and my toes sinking into the smushy zenon.

"On the new Farbie movie!!"

"Wait have you seen it yet?" I ask.

23

"Nooo no spoilers!!" Ali protests, her portal glowing pink like the color of sunrise.

I looked up at the shimmering portals, each divided into individual segments, which, when put together,that connected us all, planet to planet.

Ali came from the planet of Mar, its sublime beauty is one that I've always wanted to see, always wanted to visit. It shines like the ocean and is full of water and moons and weird enchantments that you only understand if you've lived there for at least 3 Millenia, which she has, I think she on her 8th Millenium now. and Mae OH MEA!! Her realm is one of GREEN! SPLEDID GREEN! Like the color of the trees on my planet, but every kind of green, always all at once! And her hair is one i've always envied because it flows emerald like the pothos vines, budding, though it does, in springtime. I think that's why they call her Mae, because it represents the time on her planet when the blossoms all come at once.

"I'm so sorry I'm late. I was catching lightning bugs! I love the lightning bugs they're so —"

"It's actually fireflies." Ketan said.

"Well, hold up. I have theory about that, actually."

"Mmm, yea. I think it's more of a dialectical thing." Retorted M.

Madison's realm was one that held a deep purple hue sometimes and other times it vibrated with an electric yellow. She, unlike the others, was from my home planet too. zenon. but she made the migration to Solar System 11 right after we all graduated. so fucking cool. And now she lives in mountains, at least that's what I hear. that the mountains there are wild and full and vibrating like the colors, and I heard you can see three suns there on some days. She created the group, i believe, but i'm not too sure on the lore since I was only invited like 16 subseasons ago.

"Yea, you're right. It's a dialectical thing. In the South they say lightning bugs, and in the North—"

and Ketan!! He came from the galaxy of giant floating cookies, the land of ORE-O. He has been there from the beginning. Well, from before the beginning, really. perhaps, well, I'm not even sure how long ago. But the storytelling in him runs deep, like the streams of milk that abound his homeland.

Oh and A.W. Lost in the clouds, A.W.'s planet really was. Literally. An aerial planet full of mystery. You really had to work to figure out their hieroglyphic, holographic ins and outs. but once you did, you could see it was lush with insight. delightful and cut with sarcasm. Ohhh and if you ever got a cloud dweller, like A.W. to linger for conversation, which is hard to do, as they seem to be nothing but purply blue, wispy vapor, the payoff was beyond compare. the cloud dwelling folks really are quite solid.

Which reminds me of SaM. young sam. a being like sam can talk for days and days and days. they are not a silent bunch. i swear, im not lying about that part. though not much to say of him as of late, considering his recents absence from the circle of us Evening Storytellers. Not much to say except his absence is always felt! And we wished, each fortnight, for his return. His realm, of course, was shrouded in a water-like "mystery", yet, for people there, it was all an act. A beautiful act. An amusement. but if you cracked it, like a geode maybe, you found that his people were a friendly people. My favorite kind, in fact. not much to say, but his realm was an enigma, and one that you love nothing more than to figure out.

"I love fireflies or lightning bugs or little dancing pieces of the sky! Or whatever you wanna call them!"

Ahh and VIRGIL! His realm was one of love, deep love, and of course, *adventure*. Always in his realm there were heroes. His land was the land of them. filled to the brim, as it were. Troops of them who'd fight and battle and venture together in their own narratives of intermingling friendship or companionship or rivalry. And complex splashes of courage and bright joy, too. Heroes sword fighting dragons, or vampires, or half bread vampire dragon cyclones with ink-colored eyes that would melt the soul out of you if you didn't know what you were doing. But Virgil always seemed to know what he was doing, heroically. I suppose they press that into you on his planet. There was always laughter there, and there was a generosity, or a sacredness, close to the Divine, that made it gleam the color of a seductive ember. And I always wanted to visit. But it's hard to say that I'd have the chops. I'd like to think i would. Maybe with some training. …… wait…where was Virgil tonight anyway? I didn't see his wild portal open yet.

"Me too," M laughs, "they're like aliens!"

"Wow! What a perfect Segway into our... WRITING PROMPTS!!" Mae claps her hands together, as if to gather all the wandering.

"But Virgil's not here!"

"Yes, he's, sadly, off on another adventure slaying Zorgot dragons. But don't think that means we're not storytelling tonight!"

"What's the prompt?" Ketan crumbs.

"Ali?" Mae raises her eyebrows in encouragement.

"Alians. The prompt is.... aliens."

"Alians? like from EARTH?" A.W. rains.

"The proper term would be Earthlings, and if you ask me, they're out there. The intergalactic realms of time and space are too vast for there not be some form of Earthling."

"Oki. But, I don't know. I...I don't believe... nah. I don't believe in Earthlings. eh, no way."

"But what about the footage that was just released off the Cornerstone of Engodrea! Have you watched it? You can't explain that shit," said Ali.

"Nah. Nahh"

"But ...ok, think of it this way–"

"I saw one once."

The group pauses.

"No you—"

"SAVE IT FOR THE WRITING PROMPT!" Mae cut in and another story telling night ensued, as always.

26

Prisoner from Beyond

A.W. Lowery

X-Zee (Zedd) the Invader has just returned from his campaign of Earth. He is met with fanfare and cheers from his fellow Qualvorkens. His name echoes through the streets as his ship is flanked by a royal escort on the way to the president's castle. Upon arrival, he departs his ship, and the captured prisoners are led away to the division of scientific inquiry through a service exit. He enters an inverted pyramid-shaped conference room to brief the presidents and his ministers of his findings.

President-1:

Zedd, we heard you had great success during this last campaign. You even managed to bring back prisoners.

President-2:

Yes, our science minister claims these prisoners are quite unique.

Zedd:

My Presidents, this species was quite formidable. They come in different shades of black, white and brown.

(The Science Minister stands and draws the rooms attention)

Science Minister:

I've been informed, my department has begun interrogating the prisoners. So far, our efforts have only yielded minimal results. The prisoners appear to be petrified; blankly staring at my scientists. Our best efforts to communicate have yielded no success as of yet.

Defense Minister: (pointing towards the science minister)

Have you tried torture; torture has always worked for me?

Science Minister: (glaring back)

Such primitiveness!

!!!URGENT MESSAGE!!!

Science Minister:

We have made first contact with a prisoner.

President-1 and President-2: (in unison)

What did they say?

Science Minister: ...M-O-O!!!

Terribly Terrific Ms. Tober

Virgil Thornton II

"Did you see what Ms. Tober is for Halloween?"

                                                "Eww, Ms. Tober? She's always so mean!"

"You just think that because you're always late!"

                              "Didn't she watch *Naruto* just to chat with Nate?"

                                                        "I heard she traps ghosts in her little teapot..."

"I heard if you touch her glasses, you'll rot!"

                                      "You think she's a witch? She seems so nice!"

                                                        "But I saw her talking to crows and mice!"

"You guys are stupid, all she does is read books."

                              "If you make her angry, she'll hang you from hooks!"

"Y-you're just saying stuff, that was just dumb."

                                      "She's not evil, she bandaged my thumb!"

                                      "My poem was lame, but she still gave me an A."

"She gave me two snow cones back on field day!"

                            "We forgot Cindy! You were sayin' somethin'?"

"Yeah: Ms. Tober's dressed like a *pumpkin*!"

Unsuperstitious

Samuel James

I have no superstitions.
I'm very clear of head.
Except, I guess, the ones I have
For getting out of bed.

You see, I touch my big toe down
Before the pinky goes.
Then the second, fourth, then third
May even out the row.

But don't think it unreason,
Just anatomical.
In every other earthly step
I'm purely logical.

Yes, if you see my shoes go on
Before I grab a shirt,

It's so my equilibrium
Is sure before I'm hurt.

And when I have my morning shave
While lying on my chin–
Well, I'd hate for gravity to pull
A razor toward my skin.

So don't think me irrational;
I'm quite the opposite.
Although, I guess, there is that thing
I do before I sit...

SECRET RECIPE FOR: BEGINNINGS

Curious as to how a group like this even begins? Wonder no more! M, founder of the group, shares her side here…

There is a tremendous amount of luck in the success of anything. When quarantine started in 2020, I had just graduated college and was living in the liminality of a post-grad pandemic. I missed my friends, and I missed creative writing classes, and everyone suddenly had an excess of hours in the day to fill. After many hours of commiserating with the members of this group about our shared nostalgia of regular life and in-person writing workshops, we decided to get together on Zoom to chat about writing. This was our first stroke of luck.

By the time lockdown lifted and normalcy resumed, we had spent enough time immersed in each other's minds to let go so easily. Our little writer's workshop became more than just a space to talk about our writing: it was a lifeline of sociality during an unprecedented time, and then it was our routine, a group of kids wandering the forests of adulthood together.

There is a tremendous amount of luck in finding people willing to spend an hour a week for four years (and counting) asking each other to read each other's wonderful (and sometimes awful) writing. And there is even more luck in finding a group of people so gracious and welcoming, so free of judgment and full of encouragement. Together we created a virtual space to foster creativity, to discuss our most out of pocket opinions, to consider our changing lives. Each member has chosen to dedicate themselves not only to their crafts, but to each other. In a sense, we bonded to each other, and from each other we write, and we grow. The writing that follows is a product of that bond.

BLUEBERRY

How odd it is, blue and purple on the breakfast plate... These stories are strange, ominous, mysterious, or unsettling. Chew carefully...

Employee of the Month

Ali Miller

I've won employee of the month again.

It's so nice to be appreciated. I'll hang the plaque on the wall behind me, beside the other ones. When I get off work, I'll call my mom and she'll tell me she's proud of me, and she'll mean it. I'll ride that high all the way home, watching the cornfields wind by, the only person sitting on the train because no one else's job takes them all the way out here. I'll get home and I'll order a single cupcake to be delivered to my little apartment and I'll make myself a drink and I'll go to work tomorrow and a month from now I'll be employee of the month again, just like I was last month. Just as I have been every single month since I started working here.

I don't mean to complain at all. It just feels a little silly, you see, since I'm the only person who works here. I think.

Here's the thing: it's a good job. It really is. The office is in the middle of nowhere and the first time I saw it I thought it seemed a bit small, but since I'm the only person working here it feels pretty big. I come in to work on time, and I sit down at my desk, and everything is always somehow miraculously clean. The lighting is soft, not harsh and corporate like at my last job, and since I have no coworkers, I have no complaints about their noisiness or their annoying habits. The work is straightforward and useful, and it's clear what my purpose is here. It can get a little boring, but a little boring is what I need in my life right now. This is what I wanted. It's a good job.

That's what the ad in the paper had listed it as: *A good, uncomplicated, easy job. Apply today, start tomorrow!* This was astonishing when I read it because it was exactly what I had been looking for, and because it was remarkably compelling even though I should perhaps have been suspicious. Another person might have asked questions when they got the job without interviewing at all, but I showed up to work at the time stated on my acceptance slip. That's just the kind of employee that I am. And of course, once I began working it all made sense. After all, how many qualifications do you really need to sit in a room by yourself all day and answer the occasional phone call?

At first, I thought that I worked for a front of some kind, which would have been more than fine. Three jobs previously, in fact, I was the manager of a sweet little pretzel joint that was a cover for the mafia, which I only left because I got tired of being in such an active leadership position. Then for a while I thought it might be part of a secret government operation, which I'm just not sure I could morally support, but I knew if I put my mind to it, I could get past my objections. But now I have been dissuaded of my theories. Now I know what my employers need me to do.

My first day on the job, I had simply sat in my desk chair as the hours ticked away, sweaty and anxious and uncertain. The chair was comfortable, at least, and I had allowed myself an hour and a half lunch break halfway through the day as well as a thirty-minute snack break in the afternoon, but it was altogether a very confusing first day of work. There was no welcome packet, no introductions made to the company material, and as I said, no other employees present. I stayed three minutes late, just in case some authority figure might make itself known, and went home thoroughly perplexed.

On my second day at work, my cell phone rang. I did not have a desk phone at that time.

"Hello?" I said when I answered.

"Hello," said the voice on the other end, crackling and wispy. "This is your employer."

"This is Nadia," I said, somewhat at a loss for what else to say. "It's good to hear from you."

"It is good," my employer agreed cheerfully, still in that wispy voice. "I just wanted to tell you that you're doing such a good job already. We're very glad to have you here."

"Oh, good," I said. "Can I just ask a question very quickly?"

"Of course," they said.

"What am I meant to be doing?"

"Exactly what you're doing," they said reassuringly. "Can I ask *you* a question?"

"Of course," I said.

"Is there anything that you think is...*missing* from the office? To make it feel more complete, you understand."

"Well," I said thoughtfully. "There should be a desk phone. It's only proper."

It was a nice conversation, as phone conversations go. I couldn't feel too badly about anything the whole day after we hung up. And the next morning, when I arrived at my third day of work, there was a corded phone gleaming on my desk. I smiled when I saw it, and any discomfort I had been harboring faded away like a dream. After that I settled easily into the work. I look very suitable behind a desk, and I am very good at answering the phone.

My employer is a bit old-fashioned. I get the impression that they are wealthy, aloof, perhaps of an older generation. They try their best to do the appropriate research before setting out on new ventures, but it's hard for them to understand the foreign technology. That's why they have me.

I run my fingers over my shiny gold plaque, identical to the last seven plaques that I have received, and my desk phone rings.

"Hello, Nadia," says my employer. "This is your employer."

"Yes, I know," I say. "I have the number saved in the phone's directory." This is true, but even if I didn't, I would still have made an educated guess. My employer is the only person who ever calls this phone.

"This is why you are employee of the month," they say, and I can't help myself from preening just a little. "It's the way you take initiative that really impresses me."

"I try my best," I say modestly.

"Your presence here is so crucial to our invasion of Earth," my employer says.

"Thank you so much," I say, and I find that I am genuinely touched. "I try my best. I really consider you all my family, you know."

Heed, Sapling

Maeghan Klinker

A thousand, thousand lifetimes ago, when the stones were soft and the sky was new and the rivers first tasted the sea, the Great Forests ruled in endless swathes of green. They say there were others, once, but if there were, their names are long lost to the earth, returned again to the soil and buried with the tongues that knew their shape. All that stand now are the remnants. The old growth that refused to fall beneath the ax; the woods too remote and inhospitable to bow to any invader.

You know their names already. The Tanglewood, which holds its secrets close. The Candlewood, with its burning heart and dancing shadows. The Hollowwood, which swallows all that steps beneath its branches. The Thornwood, whose thirst cannot be slaked. And the Ironwood, with bark to rival steel.

Go on, lean back. Notice the tender roughness of bark against your skin. Press your hands to its sides. What do you feel? 'Bark,' you will say. Don't be clever. Tell me now, what else? It is a soft sort of warmth radiating from the heartwood. It is why the trees of the Candlewood are furred with moss, even in the harshest snows. Why the villages of the Candlewood have no need for fires but build their homes right into the hollowed trunks of living trees. It is the magic of this place: warmth that does not burn, heat that does not suffocate.

I have been to the five forests, or what is left of them, and I tell you now that the Candlewood is the kindest of them. Plant your roots here, child, and you will live content. But you are restless as a downy milkweed seed blown on the wind. You will not know contentment until you have stepped beneath each canopy, seen the endless plains where man has felled all the great trees and raised cities in their place. I understand. I was much the same.

Heed, sapling, and I will tell you of the forests that still stand.

I was born in the Tanglewood, in a canopy-village you will not have heard the name of. We lived deep in the woods and few travelers found their way to us. When I told my mother of my decision to leave, she blessed me and told me that the Tanglewood would swallow my path and I would never come back. I didn't believe her then, but I was a young fool.

The Tanglewood is dense, filled with creeping vines and hidden dells. Strange lights and shadows flit between the trees. Do not follow them. Few are harmless, and all of them want something from you. Be sure to mark your path. The trails of that wood have a tendency to twist and double-back until you have walked ten thousand steps without moving a mile. This is the secret of the Tanglewood—it is jealous; it will try to keep you there.

If you make it from the grasp of the Tanglewood, you might think the Hollowwood an easier reprise. You would be wrong. The Hollowwood is tricksy and cunning, spreading thick moss over pits and falls, draping vines over gaping caves, waiting to catch the unaware. Roots snake across the ground, lying in wait to drag their hapless prey down to the hallowed center. If you do not mind your step, you might find your feet sinking into soft earth, swallowing you down quicker the more that you struggle. Do not fight it. Breathe slow and think quick, for the Hollowwood cares only for the clever. Knock on wood, if you must, but only as a last resort. In the Hollowwood such sound carries far. You never know what might answer.

Should you emerge from the Hollowwood, the Thornwood lies just to the east. You'll want to invest in proper attire beforehand. See this scar? And this? And this? All courtesy of the Thornwood. Yes, the eye too. Do not bother going if you are not prepared to shed a little blood. Every plant that grows in that wood thirst for it, draws it forth with needles and thorns. You cannot breathe without some prickling spine burrowing beneath your skin. But if you are prepared to walk ten thousand miles repenting each step, to inure yourself to the bite and the sting, then the fruit that grows in that wood—once you have wrested it from spiny skins and spiky shells—is the finest you will ever taste. And perhaps in a moment of beleaguered rest, you might notice that the birds that live there sing sweeter than any others, so that your agonies are accompanied by the loveliest music. One might lose themself in the Thornwood—it is a place of wretched ecstasies.

Assuming you leave the Thornwood—which is not at all a safe assumption, you know—then the Ironwood is the only forest left unknown to you. If you were wise, you would leave it that way. The Ironwood is as cold as the Candlewood is warm. It is dark and open beneath its canopy, for the trees that grow there reach far above and swallow all the light. There is no dead wood to light a fire and no sense in trying to chop any. The bark of those trees will shatter any blade. In the old days, to fell the Ironwood trees people laced the ground with poison. It was a slow death, and ugly, and the trees that remain remember this. There is no kindness in the Ironwood, no warmth and little to recommend it. But if you have come so far, have seen the light stain the leaves of each remnant canopy, you will not wish to leave the final forest undiscovered.

Take heed, sapling. To survive the Ironwood, you must bring with you torches and resin to carry light, a flint and steel for spark. Do not rest in the darkness, child. Do not trust the trees. They whisper lies and hide hungering teeth. Sleep during the day, if you must, when the light that reaches the forest floor is pale and gray-green. Journey at night, in the light of your torch for the creatures of the Ironwood will fear its flame. This is all the wisdom I can offer you. Each must find their own path through that wood. Be sure not to lose yourself along the way.

I have told you what I know of the Great Forests, and now all that is left to offer you is this: the blessing my mother gave me, passed on to you in turn. Come here, child. Let me rest my hand upon your brow. There. I can hear the words in my mother's voice as clear as the day she said them. Perhaps you will carry this piece of me with you as well.

May your path lie clear before you and your feet find steady ground. Grow strong, sapling, but not rigid, lest the winds of change cast you down. Remember that from this same living earth all dying things grow. No matter how far you wander, our roots lie tangled deep below. And at the end of all things, when the hungry earth calls you home, may your bones rest gently in the shade and the forest hold you close.

Humanity's Final Mistake

Virgil Thornton II

The trio rounded the corner to yet another hallway lined with treasure, skeletons run through with swords, gold and jewels splayed under shriveled corpses, long-dried blood speckling the carpets and low-hanging chandeliers.

At the end of the hallway, wreathed in floating candles, was a waterfall of mist. Soft organ music floated from behind it, each key shooting ice through their veins. A necromantic veil - their otherworldly quarry just beyond.

"We're coming up on him."

"Yeah Ty, the ominous organ music was a pretty big tell."

"Reloading..."

"Haven't used any grenades yet. This run's looking good, boys."

"Can't we wait for others? Take him on as a big group?"

"Miles... no one else is coming."

"Okay, well, do we have any repair kits?"

Miles looked expectantly at Jay and Tyson. The two of them busied themselves rechecking ammo and skimming readouts.

"How many repair kits did you bring, Jay?"

"... didn't bring any."

"Tyson?"

"Likewise."

"What if they get hurt? What if they have families?!"

"It's a waste of carrying capacity, kid. The Count's too fast. Tyson can tell you. We either beat him one and done or it's over."

Miles looked at Tyson, but the latter didn't return his gaze. The three stood in somber silence for a moment. It was always unnerving when Jay stopped being sarcastic.

"Alright. If we fail, the least we could do is go to their funerals."

"...I find the idea of them even *having* funerals absurd-"

"That's enough, you two. Let's move."

Tyson started off at a running crouch, and the others followed in step. They sped down the hallway, ignoring fallen heroes of old and riches untold, their sub-machine guns half-raised. Before they could second-guess themselves, they trudged through cascading fog and entered the throne room of the Great Count.

AH. VELCOME BACK.

Gunfire danced to life, filling the chamber with deafening crashes and blinding flashes of light. The vampire, an 8-foot-tall looming menace of a man, whirled forward from his organ in a rush of muscle and silk. The battle was a fierce one, the armed trio tucking and rolling, shooting and throwing grenades, while the Count slashed and kicked and thundered about.

Jay was the first to go down. The Count's claws shredded the front side of his body to ribbons, launching him high enough to slam into the ceiling. By the time he hit the floor, he had disintegrated into metal ash and carbon goo.

Next was Miles, who got a knife into the Count's shoulder before the vampire's boot slammed into his chest and out the other side. The young soldier let out an agonized, horrified wail before he too dissolved and melted.

Tyson, cornered and desperate, roared with rage and despair, spraying bullets with reckless abandon. They shattered stained glass and sent goblets flying, ricocheted off wrought-iron wreaths and splintered cobwebbed tables.

The Count was before him, and suddenly, the soldier was disarmed. Before he could grab a grenade and end them both, he was pinned to the marble floor. He tried to fight back, but the vampire's strength was beyond comprehension.

YOU HUMANS SICKEN ME VITH VAT YOU HAVE BECOME.

"Look who's talking, you undead freak."

AH, BUT IT IS THE ACCEPTANCE OF DEATH THAT SETS ME APART. I DO NOT HIJACK THE MINDS OF ANDROIDS AND FORCE THEM AROUND LIKE PUPPETS, DO I?

Tyson had no reply. He hated that part of the job. But if they didn't do it, they would have been dead several runs ago. At least this way, their team could have multiple chances to re-strategize and make progress. But the fear and pain of the droid as it died... the visceral emotion that Tyson could feel and even empathize with... that, he can never get over.

YOU MUST BE TRYING TO JUSTIFY IT IN THAT LIVING BRAIN OF YOURS. OR ARE YOUR ACTIONS FINALLY CATCHING UP TO YOU? YOU MUST DECIDE IF MACHINES ARE LESS THAN PEOPLE, HUMAN. ARE THEY JUST TOOLS, OR HAVE THEY EVOLVED INTO SOMETHING ELSE?

Tyson tapped into the emergency strength reserves. If he could just activate his grenade and keep the Count this close, he could bring him down. For all his slashing and fighting, the vampire had taken more damage in this battle than any of the previous. They were so close to victory.

The bionic muscles of the android whirred and creaked against the power of the Count. Tyson managed to get his hand 6 inches from the detonation button before the Count tore his arm from its socket. Tyson could feel his hope drain away and vibrant agony shriek to life in its place. The vampire smiled at him as he screamed.

"What now?! Are you going to keep it up with the freshman year philosophy lesson? Or are we going to kiss?"

He headbutted the Count. It was like headbutting a brick wall.

HOW PASSIONATE. FOR TOO LONG, YOU HUMANS HAVE BEEN USING ANDROIDS TO CLEAN UP YOUR NECROMANTIC MISTAKES. BUT VAT IF I DON'T KILL YOU AND SEND YOU BACK TO YOUR COZY LITTLE CONTROL ROOM? VAT IF... I BREAK THE CYCLE?

Amongst his dizziness and the pounding pain of his missing arm, Tyson barely felt it. But all the same, four fangs sink deep into the android's throat... and the world changed forever.

News19 Storm Broadcast W1/DH6 (NT)

Virgil Thornton II

STUDIO, MELISSA : It's going to stay around 29 degrees even into Friday, and those winds just keep picking up so make sure to stay inside and stay warm folks. Like we said earlier, keep the tap on so your pipes don't freeze over, and make sure you have bottled or filtered water ready in case of an outage. Stay away from windows and monitor your yard for falling debris if you have any tall trees or power lines nearby.

STUDIO, BILL : That's right Melissa, and of course this goes without saying, please keep your doors and windows *closed* and *locked* folks, and make absolutely sure your little ones are inside. This just in from NOAA: if your lights go out, do *not* light candles. That may be our first instinct, but not with this kind of storm ladies and gentlemen.

STUDIO, MELISSA : Studies show that lighting candles during mid-winter storms increases wind speeds and precipitation intensity by anywhere from 3% to as much as 61%. This is due to a phenomenon called 'primordial agitation', which scientists over at NOAA have been studying since 2001. They say this sort of reaction in the atmosphere is completely natural and dates back to before the Middle Ages but has been worsened due to climate change.

STUDIO, BILL : NOAA suggests using cell phones and battery-powered flashlights. Make sure those are plugged in to a surge protector folks. Now we're going to head over to Jerry Davidson with an On-The-Scene (*OTS*) look at tonight's storm.

[*transition*]

OTS, JERRY : ... THANKS BILL. YEAH WE'RE HERE A FEW MILES OUTSIDE OF ETERNICA AND AS YOU CAN SEE, IT'S PRACTICALLY SLEETING SIDEWAYS, WE HAD TO GET BEHIND THIS AWNING JUST BECAUSE OF THE WINDS HERE, READING MAXES OF 115 MILES AN HOUR, YOU REALLY DON'T WANT TO BE OUT HERE FOLKS. THE PARKA I'VE GOT ON IS THE SAME THEY WEAR IN ANTARCTICA BUT I CAN STILL FEEL THE–

[*thunder*]

OTS, JERRY : –SN'T GOING TO HELP MUCH ... WAIT ... I THI ... WE'RE SEEING SOME–

[*rolling thunder*]

OTS, JERRY : FOLKS I ... WE'VE GOT SOME HORSE-SHAPED FORMATIONS IN THOSE LIGHTNING STRIKES THERE, THAT'S A TELLTALE SIGN OF PRIMORD–"

[*deafening thunder*]

STUDIO, MELISSA : ...Jerry?

STUDIO, BILL : Is Jerry there?

OTS, JERRY : [*reverent, inaudible*]

STUDIO, BILL : ...did you catch that?

STUDIO, MELISSA : I think the signal got cut over near where they are. It really is dangerous so please make sure to stay indoors.

OTS, : COME OUTSIDE.

STUDIO, MELISSA : Did you hear...?

STUDIO, BILL : Who was that? No, that was static.

STUDIO, MELISSA : ...right.

STUDIO, BILL : Sorry folks, I think we're still getting feedback from Jerry's mic. Crossing signals.

STUDIO, MELISSA : Just a moment here as we–

OTS, : JERRY RIDES WITH US, AND YOU SHALL TO. WITH THUNDER UNDERHOOF AND THE LIGHTNING AS YOUR REIGNS. RIDE WITH US, YOU FOOLHARDY. DRINK OF ICE AND RAIN, FEAST O–

We at News19 apologize for the technical difficulties. We will be back on air momentarily. Tune in to 1900AM to hear the news via radio.

Starship Entity

Ketan Pandya

The starship creaked ceaselessly as he made his way through the abandoned corridors.

He had been traveling in deep space when he had come across a distress signal. When he followed it, he came across what seemed to be a derelict freighter. It seemed to be drifting aimlessly but otherwise looked intact from its cargo pods to its radiation shielding. No one answered his hails. Despite this, he saw that the hangar bay was open. He flew in, the tractor beam pulling his ship into place. He was just a traveler not a combat specialist, but he took his bolt cutter with him. One couldn't be too safe.

He entered through the hangar. The ship looked remarkably normal. The auxiliary power wasn't activated, the lights were full on, and all of the life support systems seemed to be working. Not even the security system had been activated. The only thing missing was the crew. As he made his way further in, he found the captain's console. He turned it on.

"PLEASE ENTER THE STATUS OF THE CAPTAIN." He entered "UNKNOWN" into the console.

"AFFIRMATIVE. CAPTAIN IS PRESUMED DECEASED. VIEW CAPTAIN'S LOG?" Of course he pressed yes. A video of the captain suddenly started playing.

"Whoever you are, if you are on the ship right now you have to leave. The entity...it's always there, you can feel it reaching at the edges of your vision, at the edges of your mind. I repeat, get out of there as fast as poss-" The video cuts short there. As he wonders what entity the captain could be talking about, he sees a shadow in his peripheral vision. He turns to look at it, but nothing is there. Nerves start to kick in and he starts to turn toward the corridor he came from. That's when the screaming begins.

That Which Roams the Night

Maeghan Klinker

The cracked bell in the old tower tolled dolorously as the wind shifted. It was nigh upon the witching hour and mist lay thick and curled about the headstones in the old kirkyard. A shadow, dark and pacing, flickered beneath the light of the waning moon. The church grim, keeping its faithful watch. The branches of the old elm creaked and moaned in the wind, and beneath its mournful gaze the restless dead began to stir. Tip sat crouched in the long grass at the edge of the graveyard, his limbs stiff with cold and his breath forming phantom clouds before his face. He wished Mab would hurry up.

Tip shivered in the dark, counting headstones to distract himself from the chill. A cloud shrouded the frost-tinged moon and in the half-light, Mab appeared, looking cross and sour, her arms crossed irritably over her shawl. "Thomas Mahony," she snapped. "I thought I told you to keep away from here."

Tip scowled at his older sister and started up out of the grass, stumbling with pins and needles. "You're dead, Mab," Tip argued. "That makes me the oldest now. You can't boss me around no more."

"You wish," she scowled. "Besides, you're still a month short of thirteen. I'm your elder sister yet. You ought to mind my words."

Tip rolled his eyes. "Don't see why I should. You're no wiser than the day you passed."

Mab narrowed her eyes at him. "Mam know you're out?"

Tip scoffed. "Course not."

"Then maybe I ought to appear before her, apparition like, and let her know what a dalcop son she bore. Don't you know what time of the year it is?" she scolded testily. "You shouldn't be–"

Mab whipped her head to the side and froze, standing with such complete stillness, eyes unblinking, that it raised the hairs on the back of Tip's neck. When she was nagging at him, it was easy to forget she was dead and buried, but it was harder now, with her staring eyes and rigor mortis posture.

"Mab?" Tip prompted uneasily.

The truth was—though he'd never tell her, lest she be unbearably smug about it—he missed his sister. Since she'd passed, their home had become a gray and fragile thing. His trips to the graveyard were some of the only times he remembered what laughter tasted like or how a smile was supposed to fit on his face. Since he'd first discovered his sister's ghost, he'd never been afraid of her. It was just Mab, and Mab would never hurt him. But this stillness was unsettling.

Looking around, Tip realized that the mist in the graveyard had gotten thicker, but it no longer swirled and shifted, instead hanging oppressive and still as Mab. Tip was about to speak his sister's name again when her eyes grew big and frightened. "They're coming," she whispered. She turned to Tip, frantic. "Go home, Tip. Be sure to bar the door with iron. Quickly!"

Tip stepped back, startled by her sudden intensity. "Who's coming?"

A sound rose in the distance. A strong wind, Tip thought, bending the trees. A distant howl. Mab flickered in fear before him. "Now, Tip!" she commanded in her bossiest big sister voice, and on habit Tip's feet started stumbling homeward at her tone. "Run home, and don't look back!"

The wind tore at Tip as he ran, seeming to come from all directions. The sound grew closer. A roar. The baying of hounds. A high, clear horn.

Too late, Tip remembered that it was not yet twelfth night. Too late, he remembered the ghost stories his eldest sister used to tell them, all the little ones huddled close beneath the blanket in the dark, of the terrible things that roamed the skies on winter nights. The Wild Hunt. Clamorous and ceaseless in their hunger.

He ran like a rabbit through the dark. For once, he minded his sister's words. He didn't look back.

He didn't look back, so he couldn't say what truly happened that night, or how a dead girl kept the Hunt distracted long enough for her brother to slip away. All he knew was that no matter how many times he snuck down to the graveyard in the days and weeks and months after, he never saw his sister's ghost again. But sometimes, particularly on cold winter nights, he thought he heard her voice high on the wind warning him to bar the door with iron. To run home, and don't look back.

The Ballad of Dirt and Moon

Ali Miller

In the end, when Dirt died, there was no funeral. This is because funerals are held for the living, and no one left alive saw any reason to celebrate her. And if the jaw was clenched a little too tight, no one questioned it. If the rigor mortis seemed to come on too suddenly, no one batted an eye. They wanted her gone.

They did bury her, if only to get the body out of sight, but even this was as insolent an occasion as they could make it. No one bothered to dig a ditch: they simply rolled the body into a pile of dark, moist soil and let it be swallowed. It was a silent affair. When they were done, they turned their backs on her. They brushed their hands clean and went to bed.

Afterwards, Moon walked the town that Dirt had razed to the ground, the place which had teemed with life and was now rubble. Her right leg had a crooked gait from where Dirt had stomped on it once (that had happened when they were children, long before the war) and a fresh hole in her left side (that one was from Dirt the night she'd died). If anyone would've had a right to ask for a grave marker, it would have been Moon. She never would have asked, but if she had they would have granted it to her. Fortunately, dirt piles make just as distinctive guides as grave markers.

Moon slowed to a stop. The pile was formless and looming in the dark of night, the sky so rich and blue that it made the disturbed ground and wreckages of buildings seem uglier by comparison. War was ugly. Death was ugly. Moon looked up at the sky briefly. Her lips moved soundlessly, and to an outsider it might have looked like she was praying, but in actuality what she was doing was working up enough moisture in her mouth to hock a truly massive loogie, which she spat derisively onto the dirt.

As it sank into the ground, a hand emerged. Moon watched passively as Dirt dug herself out painstakingly slowly, coughing every so often, cheeks streaked and jaw still clenched. When she was done, she looked up pitifully from beneath her eyelashes, trying to gauge if Moon would offer her a hand, and standing on her own when it became clear that Moon would not. She cleared her throat, spat a little to get rid of the phlegm and debris of being dead and buried. "That one was my bad," she said hoarsely, meaning the war and the destruction and the ugly death.

Moon slapped her across the face.

Dirt groaned, bent back with the force of it. "Okay," she said. "I deserved that."

With Eyes Unblinking

Maeghan Klinker

Dear Citizen,

I have seen you. 8:55 am. Running late. I saw you cross the street. Watched you step in the fresh pink bubble gum, needy and clinging, on the sidewalk. I saw you frown in disgust, scrape your shoe along the rough pavement to dislodge the menace. [zzzzzzzzz]. F and 5th. [zzz]. K and 4th. [zzzz]. L and 3rd. You pushed open the glass doors of an office building and went inside without saying goodbye.

I too have a job to do. I watch the city. I protect. I see.

I saw you.

4:48 pm. Stealing minutes where you can. It's okay. I won't tell. [zzzz.] I watch you skirt around corners with hurried steps, eager to get home. [zzz]. 3rd and L. 4th and K. 5th and F. You descend. [zzz]. I watch unblinking as you stand on the platform, shift from foot to foot. A train arrives at 10x speed, video on fast-forward. You step into its metal embrace. Disappear without saying goodbye.

I do not steal minutes. I am an accountant of hours. All the hours that pass in this city under my watchful gaze. I see the homeless man and the hot dog stand. [zzzz]. The vandal and the cop. [zzzz]. The busker and the man to toss the coin into their starving case. The spectacle of sirens and flashing lights. The drama of each small moment lived across countless lives. I do not cry.

[zz-zzzzzz] Night descends. The streetlights flicker on. I wipe the static from my eyes and blink, shifting to accommodate nearsighted night. I watch the ATMs. [zzzzz]. Record the hiss of sprayed paint and less pleasing substances against the alley walls. Watch the bubble gum spat upon the pavement.

You leave countless marks upon this world, and then turn blind eyes upon them.

But do not worry. I have kept your tally. I have seen you. I have seen you all.

Even when you do not see me.

Even though you never wave goodbye.

I wait for you, eyes unblinking,

CCTV

SECRET RECIPE FOR: LOGISTICS

We Wafflers meet weekly to practice our writing. But just what does that look like? Maeghan, the group facilitator, has something to say…

Gather round, gather round, and I shall speak of heroes. For heroes they are, those valiant writers that shrug off the 9-5, push past the exhaustion of grad school, or dig their way out from crippling doubt surrounding the future to gather together once a week and create stories.

It is true, it is a bit of a social affair. Such is the case among heroes, who must boast of the spoils of their meme-hunts and make jests at one another and run the familiar weft of old arguments through their teeth to be comforted by the predictable back-and-forth. It seems these repartees wax longer each time we meet—and it must be admitted that sometimes they are the sole object of the meeting, when creative energy is low, or the writers cannot be mustered to task. If you have ever tried to keep a group of writers on task, you will know what a challenge this is. It is second only to trying to keep a group of writers to a deadline (Ye God, have mercy).

It is a thankless job being a merciful dictator, I shall have you know, and writers are an unruly bunch.

And can you believe they've started to rate my segues? The audacity.

But writers will be audacious. Especially when you ask them to write (the scandal!). Our prompts usually fall into two categories: craft and hat. A craft prompt will focus on a specific element of the craft of writing, such as thinking about pacing or language or setting, etc. These are usually more technical and reminiscent of school (you're learning something, and your brain feels like you're learning something).

And then there are the hat prompts.

Imagine that you have a magical hat that contains every concept in the known universe, and then you reach in a hand and draw something out. Sometimes you get a prompt like, "write a story about the wild hunt," and sometimes you get a prompt like, "write a short autobiography about a multiverse version of yourself." Hat prompts are fun because everyone interprets them so wildly differently, each colored by our own voice and interests and perspectives.

Mostly, any prompt is picked with the goal of getting writers to write (surprisingly hard) and having fun (with this group, always easy). So, join us! Pick a prompt, hat or craft (there's a list in the back). Put fifteen minutes on the clock (or 20, or 30. 5 more minutes? Why not). Ready? Set. Write!

STRAWBERRY

Bright and vibrant, loud and tart. These stories are raw, emotional, violent, or manic. Have plenty of napkins, you'll get messy!

Evil

Samuel James

The enormity of evil that had transpired those years to bring the two criminals, Lady and Mr. Split, against a unit of angry lawmen, personally assembled for the purpose of their execution, was reminiscent of an older, heroic age of criminality. Bonnie and Clyde. Butch Cassidy and the Sundance Kid. Jesse and Frank James. Their charges: murder, extortion, torture, burglary—but all great criminals have the same charges. It is their style that differentiates their greatnesses.

"We've been in worse," said Lady. She knew style. She knew that death would be an important line in her history, and she was thinking about honor. She thought it was largely an exercise in posture.

"Worse?" said Mr. Split. "And did we survive it?"

Before Lady could cleverly reply, Mr. Split went on. "I guess we made it here, survived as much as that. This isn't great, though, no. This is bad, yes, bad. If surviving means ending up here, no, I'll take the other, yes."

Mr. Split was mad, and he was bleeding from the head. His odd and contradictory character, coupled with his injury, rendered him unaware of the distance between himself and reality; yet the slight confusion and hurt he could recognize, he felt to be an injustice worth true wrath. His vague world was hated. That was all the feeling he had: wrath and a childish love for Lady.

Yes, yes, we are past the age of romantic criminals. The modern-day Clyde: who could love him when he really did commit murder. And Bonnie, for all her love, was simply a bad human being. But—

But, no—and the lawmen, too, who recalled their romantic predecessors—but who can romanticize the policeman, another cog in a bureaucratic, brutalist nation of laws. The law. The law. The law comes eventually.

Even those criminals who do remember their honor, the Robin Hoods of files and finance, the hackers and redistributors of...

I think I am asking: where is the style? And can't I yearn?

There is the criminal worth my heart—not your liberal grace of god bleeding heart, but my ancient, yearning, human heart.

I understand: their rap sheet is long. It is savagery and malice that routes their story. So why do I see two murderers and think: escape. For once, escape. Why does my human heart beat against reason, against morality, for death and free evil?

Hesitation, and How to Fold Shirts

Virgil Thornton II

Hard blue lines of light bleed through the wood of the back wall, then it explodes, spraying splinters across the floor. Vice Admiral Ferrule C. Scarmaker, a tall, muscular man with heavy eyebrows and an even heavier mustache, swallows his unease and marches into the cabana. Close behind is a hailstorm of booted footsteps as sailors pour in around him, raising their rifles. The naval officer slides his greatsword into the custom scabbard along his back and pulls manacles from his belt.

"Did we interrupt your laundry? I'll get the forensics crew to throw the next load in the dryer for you."

The nymph sitting on the king-sized bed smirks. She looks like a human woman but with a fishy complexion: jet black eyes, turquoise skin and seaweed hair, spiny dorsal fins perking up where ears should be. Her hands are clasped behind her.

All around her are folded shirts and sundresses, swim trunks and blankets, beach towels and bikinis. Piles of vacation clothes are sorted in rainbows across the smooth white comforter. More clothes and fabrics are tucked neatly into the shelves along the walls. A half-empty laundry basket rests against her leg. The air smells like dryer sheets and sandy wood.

The nymph studies the men, her beady eyes causing some of them to take uncertain shuffles backward. She frowns.

"Is this about last year's taxes?"

"Panopea of Bleómous. You've killed eighty-seven people with your magic, all of which were unsuspecting tourists, and nineteen of which were children. Don't even try to deny it, we have mountains of evidence."

Her shoulders, splashed with indigo freckles, rise and fall as she shrugs.

"You must not have seen the condition they've left my beaches in. My reefs, my grottos, the filth is disgusting! And every time I clean, it just comes right back. A prudent woman would end the problem at the source, wouldn't she?"

"I'm not here to argue morality with you. Put your hands up. You're coming with us."

Scarmaker takes a menacing step forward, but Panopea doesn't budge. Her hands are still clasped behind her. She squints and smiles at the vice admiral, leaning forward. Small, white shark fangs gleam like pearls in the tropical sun.

"This hardly seems fair."

The sailors shuffle, some of their guns wavering.

Scarmaker keeps his face stern. His palms and mustache are beginning to prickle with sweat. If he needs to, he will drop these manacles and take out his blade. He can perform a Blue Thrust in two seconds flat, one-and-a-half if the damned thing doesn't get caught in his scabbard. He is a practiced swordsman. A *master* swordsman. There is no need to show fear. That is what she wants.

"We have you surrounded. Comply."

"You sound nervous, Captain."

"It's Vice Admiral. Now that's enough chatter. Surrender peacefully."

"Won't you let me grab my shawl from the basket first?"

This is how the nymph does her magic. It was briefed to them ad nauseam the days prior. Scarmaker is unamused. He takes another heavy step towards her and she squirms.

"I said that's enough."

"... ah, yes, very well."

Panopea moves her hands, but not to put them behind her head. She's pulling something out, something she's been holding and hiding this whole time. A polo shirt, part of the official field uniform that all the sailors are wearing. A sense of alarm blooms in Scarmaker's gut. The briefings said her magic is performed with a laundry basket. What could this be? Is this part of her spell?

"Stop, Panopea! Hands up, final warning!"

She lays the shirt face-down on the bed. Her webbed fingers smooth the fabric out. Scarmaker drops the manacles and his greatsword comes out in a wide, glassy whoosh. His heart is racing, eyes wide. With only a second, he's not properly poised to do a Blue Thrust, so instead he blocks diagonal and braces himself.

"SAILORS, OPEN FI-"

She pinches the sleeves of the shirt at the tops of their openings and folds them inward towards the center of the back.

The room is filled with screaming as all of the sailors' rifles clatter to the floor, their arms simultaneously forced behind them, their shoulders almost shattering under the force, chests poked out and stretched.

She takes the shirt by the bottom and the shoulder, folding it inward again. She does so on both sides so that the emblem on the back of the shirt can still be seen, but the sleeves are tucked under the previous fold.

Sailors crunch and crackle, their screams turning into gurgling groans, blood spurting from mouths as they collapse to their knees, their bones folding and snapping in unnatural ways.

She takes the bottom of the shirt by either side and makes a large fold along its middle, placing the edges she is holding by the shoulders.

Groans cease and crunches continue as the sailors' upper halves are pulverized, spines turned to mulch in even the most flexible of them.

She makes one last fold, again along the middle, pulling back the shoulders so that they rest on the crease of the previous fold.

It is overkill.

Vice Admiral Scarmaker now stands in an oozing bloodbath, his men reduced to malformed pancakes, him alone with a splattered black uniform and a trembling greatsword. He is putting his all into staying upright and holding down his vomit. He was too unsure, too lenient. He should have walked around and looked at her hands, he knew something was off, he should have listened to his gut. He should've just tackled her and cuffed her instead of jabbering about. Dammit, it is all his fault! Dammit!

Panopea plops the white polo on top of a floral sundress.

"Filthy. I'm going to have to throw the rest of this in the wash, it seems."

He could charge forth and cleave her in two. A Blue Thrust would be faster, he just needs one lunge and she'll be blasted to bits. He can do it; he has the speed and training to do it. He has to, to avenge his men, to erase this monster from the coasts of this island.

Scarmaker brings the hilt high across his chest, bracing his feet, focusing. He can do it now. The sword is heavy, but he is fast enough.

The nymph pulls out a naval officer's uniform shirt from her basket and his heart sinks. It is identical to the one he is wearing.

"This one looks clean, at least. May I fold it before your men come get me?"

His stomach is cold. Ice floods his veins. It is not the power of the Blue Thrust, but an all-encompassing fear. He stands, a child frozen before a viper. A balmy breeze wafts up the coppery scent of his men's entrails.

Invisible pressure kneads into his shoulders as Panopea begins to massage the shirt.

"You can give up, you know. I won't tell anyone."

There is a war inside him. One side is Vice Admiral Scarmaker, roaring for revenge, brazen with bloodlust, overcome by his duty to kill and fight and protect. The other side is Ferrule, a tired, scared, hollow man who just saw his friends die and wants to run home.

The nymph stops massaging the shirt and drapes it across her lap. Her smile is what ends that war. Her patient, smug, facetious smile.

This is a monster, not a criminal. For that, he was not prepared. He will be too slow. He is a coward, which was always the case. Ferrule puts his sword and cap next to the mangled bloody pulp that was his second-in-command. She deserved them more than he, after all. Defeated, he turns to exit through the wall-hole he created with his first and only Blue Thrust of the day.

"Ah ah ah~!" Panopea sings, sending dread through his heart, "Just where do you think you're going? Come sit on the bed with me. We're going to have a little… 'negotiation' about tourism on my island ♡"

How Paper Wishes Burn

Ali Miller

The room was quiet, disturbed only by the early risers—gentle susurration of one or two pairs of shears slicing through thick paper, and the occasional crackle of the fires. Timothy was better than anyone else at cutting wishes. She was faster, nimbler, more careful and precise than any of the other initiates. She normally sat quite far from the braziers, so far that by evening she was shaking in the cold and squinting in the low light, and still she could deliver an armful of wishes to the fire and be back to her chair before anyone blinked, shears slicing again like they had never stopped.

Timothy loved wishes. She loved the silliness of them, she loved the sweet-smelling and creamy paper that they came attached to, she loved the tingling starlight that lit up the room when they were burned. She loved, very distantly, the people who made them. Those people whose hearts lurched painfully in their chests; the people whose want was so powerful it took physical form. Sometimes, her love for wishes made her weep. There was nothing else in the world that mattered. Not to Timothy.

If Timothy loved wishes, then Caroline loved to hurt Timothy. He was her constant tormentor, the drilling parasite that she could not escape. Caroline had been here in this room nearly as long as Timothy. He was big and broad, with a warm laugh and a faint woody scent that reminded Timothy of wish paper, and he was sharp tongued and never far behind her. When she ate he would line her bowl with ash, so she had stopped eating. When she slept he would whisper mockingly in her ear, so she had stopped sleeping. There was nothing he had not tried to take from her, except for wishes.

Today he pulled back a chair beside him, up close with the popping fire and the soft murmuring laughter of other initiates trickling into the room, and beckoned her towards him. Timothy clutched her armful of wish paper and stared. Caroline rolled his eyes impatiently and jerked his chin towards the chair. The gesture was clear. Timothy was deeply uncertain. She went over on stumbling feet, but did not speak.

"Sit down," said Caroline. Timothy did not sit. "Sit *down*," he said again, "I saved this seat specifically for you. Don't you appreciate it?"

Timothy sat. Caroline smiled at her. "There you go," he said. "Attagirl. Isn't that nice? Doesn't the fire feel good?"

Timothy shrugged. He nodded. "Put your hands out," he coaxed. "Isn't it warm?"

Timothy set the wish paper carefully in her lap. She reached her hands out cautiously. It was so warm. Her hands had never felt like this before, hot and prickling. It felt like burning wishes. Was it supposed to feel this good? Some of the others were murmuring with surprise in the background. She sat back, eyeing Caroline, who was watching her with a dangerous, satisfied expression. Her shoulders tensed with anticipation, but all he did was snap his shears across a sheet of paper. She smoothed out her own wishes and began to cut. At first, she paused periodically to check Caroline, but he was silent and sturdy beside her, working easily. Eventually she fell into the meditative rhythm.

She was even faster from this seat, she found. She didn't need to pause to carry her wishes across the room. She didn't need to breathe hot air onto her frozen fingers to keep them moving. She could feel that her cheeks were ruddy with the pleasure of wish work and it was almost wonderful. She was tense, though. When the lunch bell chimed, she jumped in her seat, startled.

Timothy stood and pocketed her shears. The part of her that knew Caroline well, that understood him deeply, that part of her was whispering that she should savor this, that she might never have it again. She didn't want to let her guard down. But she wanted the warmth of the fire to last. She tipped her face forward, just a little, and closed her eyes to savor it one last time. With her eyes shut, she couldn't see it coming when Caroline shoved her from behind.

For a moment, she felt weightless. Then, against her cheek, the shock of pain when the bone connected with the thick metal edge of the brazier, the tingling rush of a burn where the fire touched her sensitive skin. She landed on the stone floor and skidded her palms against it. When she opened her eyes, soft white paper ash was floating in the air around her and Caroline was brushing off his hands, looking down at her prone on the ground. The brazier was tipped over, embers spilling out of the bowl, scattered all across the floor. The ornately scrolled stand that it had rested upon was on its side next to her.

"You're so *pathetic*," he laughed, watching her chin tremble. Everyone was staring.

She picked herself up, hands shaking. Caroline's face was sharp and pleased and handsome. Timothy wanted it bloody, wanted it ripped and torn and twisted in pain. She wanted him to burn. Timothy clutched her fists, knuckles white, and leapt forward, beating wildly against any part of him that she could reach.

"Whoa, whoa," he said, stumbling back. Timothy was panting hard. She wiped soot and sweat from her face and shifted her weight. Her toe kicked against the brazier stand where it still lay and she bent to pick it up, handling it thoughtfully. She tested the heft of it with both hands. Caroline looked from the metal to her face. His hands went up to defend himself, but it was too late. She swung.

The heavy bronze met his skull with a dull thud that rang up her arms and through her body. She watched, detached, as his legs buckled and he collapsed to the ground. He groaned faintly and did not move, but Timothy knelt and pinned him down with her whole weight just to be safe. A single piece of wish paper was trapped beneath his head, with his hair fanned out around it like a halo. There was blood staining the paper. Something dug into her hip where she was bent over—her shears, in her pocket. She pulled them out, fingers curled around the handles. Firelight glinted off the sharp tip.

"Oh, have a heart," Caroline said. His beautiful mouth was half-smiling, eyes disbelieving. She stared down at him, one knee still pressed to his throat, gently forcing his head back so that he strained to hold it up.

"Very well," Timothy said, and his shoulders relaxed. "I shall have yours," and brought the shears down.

In The Winter, She Baked

M Sweezy

"YES, CHEF" The kitchen yells in unison. Cherry, the sous, whips around and inspects the line.

"Sloppy work, Terry. Who taught you to whisk, your mother? Was she an invalid, Terry? Was she in a terrible accident that cost her the feelings in her elbows? She must have been an invalid to have a technique as shite as that. Get that out of my kitchen, get that the hell out of my kitchen. Start again."

"Lord have mercy, what is this? What the actual fuck is this, Jom? A crème brûlée? At 10 in the goddamn morning? If I wanted my mouth fucked I'd hire a whore, you fucking oaf." Cherry spits filthy at Jom's face as she runs one swift, chef's hand across Jom's station. Pots and pans clamber to the floor, spilling sugar and cinnamon and good lord is that a split egg yolk? Jom never stood a chance.

At the table next to Jom's, Sugarpie moves slowly. It's not in the business of kitchen staff to move slowly. Especially not in Chef's kitchen. See, the whole point is to move quickly. Quickly and angrily, and with enough cortisol in your body to kill a small child. That's what cooking is, after all. Anger, stress, and yelling so loud you lose feeling in your tastebuds.

But Sugarpie doesn't cook. Sugarpie bakes. Sugarpie writes memories and hands them to you on a plate, spins a pretty little story that you forgot you heard and watches as, with each bite, you remember. Cherry eyes Sugarpie's station: clean, organized, promising. She makes a snide remark that does not reach wherever Sugarpie's mind is, and she walks on.

In the absence of yelling, Chef turns. Chef walks towards Sugarpie, and Sugarpie doesn't notice. Sugarpie is in her mother's kitchen in the winter of 1973. Chicago winters were harsh back then, harsher than even now if you can believe it. They didn't have much, a couple pairs of socks if they were lucky, a good coat with no holes if they were blessed. But Sugarpie's mom was always baking. She got the itch for it in the winter, see. She was one of those women who can't stand still, not ever. Hands always twitching, looking for a baby to cradle, a heart to sooth, a forehead to kiss. In the spring she was out planting, in the summer she was dragging those kids to every free event the city would offer, making up stories about princes and frogs and ogres and beasts. She sang sweet melodies she said she learned from the stars. But in the winter, she baked.

Now Sugarpie, she could eat anything. She wasn't picky, no one was back then. She ate what she was given and she liked it. But she loved her mom's baking, and she especially loved her mom's famous red velvet cupcake. It sat stark in her memory like a drop of blood on snow. She likes to keep things like that, nestled in her mindspace, secret only to her. She wouldn't usually attempt necromancy, bringing back this memory that has long since been buried. She wouldn't normally, except for–

Chef's eyes were like those Chicago winters. Cold, harsh, but with the promise of spring just behind them. Those icy eyes stared down at her now. Sugarpie looked everywhere, except into that winter. She looked at the chin sharp like Chef's knives, arms lean and hidden under those white robes, fingers strong with veins running down them like rivers, running into the hand that was slowly reaching for Sugarpie's creation.

Prisoner Number Twelve

Ali Miller

The water was coming in around the bars of her cell, waves lapping at the rusty metal and depositing soft brown sand on the concrete underneath her toes. Prisoner Number Twelve sat passively on her bed and watched the tide rise around her. From the bed in the cell next to her, the only other sea-facing cell, Prisoner Number Five coughed weakly. The salt air did not agree with her the way it did Number Twelve.

"Shut the fuck up," Number Twelve said.

"Beg pardon," Number Five said mildly, and coughed gently again.

The tide came crawling in, as always.

Most people understood the rising tide as a sudden enemy, a trick of the ocean—one moment it was far out, a sliver of sparkling light in the distance, and the next it had climbed up around your ankles and cut you off from your exit. Not Number Twelve. She had sat here for so long, on blankets that never fully dried, watching the tide inch its way inwards. She understood it like a lover. It was slow and patient and reliable. It would not abandon her.

Twelve's face was wind-rough and she had been trapped in this little cell long enough that some might say she had begun to go mad. Those people did not understand the intimacy that Twelve shared with the thick layer of sand atop her concrete cell floor. They did not know about the snails that wobbled around her feet, burrowing in her footsteps and attempting to massacre her toes. They couldn't see the barnacles growing on barnacles growing on barnacles. One day, if she didn't get out of this damp shell-crusted prison cell, she would grow barnacles too.

From the cell next to her, the only other occupied cell that she knew of, the only other living prisoner on this algae-soaked hellhole, came a stifled cough, tearing Twelve out of her gentle, meditative thoughts. She cut her eyes in the direction of the other cell as though Number Five could feel the weight of her irritated gaze.

"Shut the fuck up," she said.

Five muttered an apology, and halfway through it coughed again.

"I said SHUT UP," Number Twelve roared, and in dizzy anger picked a chunk of loose concrete off the floor of her cell and chucked it through the bars into Number Five's. It slammed into her forehead, knocking her head back with its force and sending her into hacking fit of further coughing. Twelve groaned, sat back down, put her head in her hands. She tried desperately to focus on anything else—the slamming of the waves against stone, her own heartbeat, the wailing wind.

"Ouch," said Five raspingly, when she had finally caught her breath.

"I am so sick of you," Twelve snapped.

"I know."

"I am sick to death of you. I am tired of being damp. I want to be alone again."

"You wouldn't be more yourself without me. You'd just be alone."

"What does that even mean?"

"You'd miss me," Twelve promised.

"I'd rather miss you and be rid of you then!" she screamed, and fell silent.

She watched the waves beat at the iron bars keeping her trapped in this little space. The bars were eroding faster than she had expected. The architect had not accounted for the clever fingers of the ocean. Every new high tide, she walked a miserable, eroded step closer towards freedom. Twelve was patient. She had waited this long. She was willing to wait a little longer.

The walls and floor shook with the rolling of the rocks against the jetty wall on which their little prison perched. Neither prisoner flinched. They had both been locked inside so long that they were used to it.

"I will destroy you if I can," Number Twelve promised Five. She lay back on her tiny damp bed and closed her eyes against the ever-present gray light of the sky.

"I know you will," said Number Five. "And I will show you mercy. Again and again and again."

Restless Cleo

M Sweezy

Birds get restless before migration. They can't stand still. They become little balls of feathers and cortisol and flit so endlessly on their feet, flap so endlessly on their wings. The only thing that brings them back to sanity is flying to the other side of the world.

Cleo has always been like a bird right before migration.

Even as a kid her hands wouldn't stay still by her side. Once she screwed the nails out of her crib walls, fell off the edge onto the big, ugly rug her parents had put in her room, and crawled right to the kitchen. She learned to run before she ever walked. The school held her back three years because she wouldn't stay in her seat. Track team kicked her off because she'd get bored at practice. People thought she was stupid, crazy, mentally inept. Her parents didn't know what to do with her, so she ran. Like any restless heart, she loved to love. She plunged into relationships just as quickly as she pulled out of them. Cleo lived at 2x speed, and the world was blurred around her.

In all her life, there's only one thing that Cleo stuck with. A little baby whose fingers never fiddled with the screws, whose calm golden eyes stared into the restless ocean of her mothers', whose laugh could stop a bird on its path.

***

Most people are in it for the money. Jobs get scarce and life gets shitty, and money is the shining golden spotlight of a better tomorrow. If Cleo lied to herself, she could believe that she wasn't like those people. If she really needed to, she could get an office job, get a button-down suit, put the baby in daycare and drain her soul from 9-5 every day for the rest of her life. If she lied to herself, she could believe she was in it for the adventure, for the thrill, for the romance of it all. If she was better at lying, or better at believing, maybe she wouldn't be in this mess.

In the head of a restless, ruthless, flighty brain, compartmentalization is the key to survival. Baby needs food, food requires money, Cleo gets the money. The rationalization was easy at first, when she was still a young petty thief with dirt-caked nails and a stomach that wouldn't stay full. Sunburnt tourists, with their overflowing pockets and wine-stained nativity, made an easy target. They flung money around so carelessly Cleo didn't even have to change the narrative in her head—surely they could find another bracelet, buy another wallet when they got home. But Cleo got too good for her own good, those flying hands of hers had been practicing since birth. They noticed her, they called her into a meeting. They didn't even have to threaten her, that's how desperate she was. And really in the grand scheme of things, when we're all worm food, what's the difference? What's the difference between grifting a few credit cards and stealing the golden coffin of Nedjemankh?

It got easier the richer she got. Suddenly the baby was chubby and glowing and the brand-new cotton onesies sat perfectly on her little body. Cleo found out she looked stunning in gold, and pair it with a slinky black dress from the Italian magazines, she could get free drinks and a meal to go from any man on the street. She got used to coming home to their nanny, who showered the baby in kisses and made them both home cooked meals. Cleo got rich, but her desperation never settled.

It's just a coffin, she'd tell herself at night. She never was good at lying.

The Lamplighter

Maeghan Klinker

The sun was just beginning to set as Gadget capered over the Hills of Lost Worth, the rusted detritus of past lives skirling down the towering heaps beneath his feet and tumbling into the shifting valleys below. He had been busy getting ready for night. A busy, busy time. The busiest, when you were Gadget. The hills stretched on for as far as the horizon could reach. They said, once upon a time, back in the old days, that hills were green, or purple, or blue, and covered in things called trees which were like lampposts only if they had lots of arms and no lights at all, which, Gadget thought, meant they weren't really like lampposts at all. There were lots of lampposts in the Hills of Lost Worth. Gadget made sure of it. Of course, they hadn't all started out life as lampposts. That was the very best thing about the hills. Everything that wound up there was worthless until it was made into something else. Gadget hadn't been worth spit on a boot when he'd shown up, and now look! He laughed to himself as he gamboled up a steep slope, a scree of old coins and aluminum cans and a half bald tennis ball and old boots tumbled in his wake.

 Now Gadget was the Lamplighter. All the lampposts of Lost Worth were his. His chest puffed out with pride. His, his, his. He had made them. Made them of all sorts of things. Things no one wanted. No one but him. He smiled as he reached his next light. It was an easy one. The front half of an old machine jutted from the cliff face. The red paint was chipped and mottled with rust, the glass pane at its front completely absent except for a few stubborn shards thirstily waiting for blood. Gadget tutted at them reprovingly as he swung into the inside of the machine. It took a little finagling, but with the help of a few twisted wires, there was a sharp zapping sound and then one of the headlights flickered to life, shining out across the mounds of wilted treasure.

Gadget let out a joyful whoop. The light buzzed through him, lit up his insides like a whole forest of lampposts. He had made the light, and the light was his. It shone for him, pointing him towards his next charge. He scampered out of the car and slid down the slope, following the faint beam of the headlight. The sky was turning a dusky purple now, and if he didn't hurry, he would have to call his lights up in the dark.

He went faster, but not too fast. There were dangers in this kingdom of treasures. Hidden edges, sharp and greedy, iron bars that dreamed of being lances, hungry creatures with mean smiles that longed for a taste of Gadgets. But these things didn't show their faces in the light. Nothing would dare touch his lights. No, no, no, not *his*. He panted as he reached his next lamppost. This one was a bit tricksy and required feeding. Gadget rooted around in the many pockets of his clothes and the pouches of his belt. There had to be something there, something he could feed the light. The setting sun clawed at him like a frantic thing, his hands twitching and clumsy as they rummaged through his pockets.

Where was it? What was it? Where and what and what and where, oh *where* was it? His fingers brushed against a soft crinkle. His breath whooshed out of him in relief as he pulled the tattered twist of paper towel from the pocket inside of the pocket inside the left sleeve of his coat. It was mottled and moldy and more stain than not, but it was dry now and that's what mattered. Gadget crawled along a large length of pipe until he reached the end. Then he leaned over the edge and peered inside, waiting for his eyes to adjust to the dark. One time, he had found a crouching, mangy bobcat hissing and spitting when he'd come to light this lamp. As his eyes adjusted to the gloom, he spotted the bobcat's skull gaping in the shadows, a warning to any other creature that came there: this lamppost was *his*. All that the light touched. His, his, his.

Scooching past the skull, he crawled through the scummy ooze at the bottom of the pipe until he reached the lamppost. It was an old oil lamp, only one pane cracked and still 1/3 full of oil after Gadget had topped it up with what could be gleaned from the bobcat. It took a bit of knowing to get it to light though. Gadget tore off a bit of the paper towel and carefully twisted it up and wound it about with a piece of string until only a very teensy bit of paper towel stuck out the top. He laced this makeshift sort of wick into the oil lamp then rummaged about in his many pockets until he found a cracked and faded lighter.

Gadget was an expert at sparks, which were just really tiny lampposts that fizzled out before they could be his, and within seconds the wick caught and the lamppost guttered and flared, adding its smoky yellow light to the dim pipe. Gadget laughed and slithered back the way he came. He turned to admire his work. The pipe was cracked in several places, and the glow of the lamppost within made it look like an artery to the heart of the earth, hidden and secret and his, all his. Gadget spun to gaze upon the constellation of lights trembling over the Hills of Lost Worth. Pulsing neon and glaring LED and flickering flame and twinkling strings and blinding floodlights and twirling lighthouses, all brought to life by his hand. All the light touched, his. His heart swelled until he absolutely screamed with joy. The sound echoed over the towering hills of rust, bouncing and distorting strangely across the piles of junk until it was swallowed by the night. Of course all this was his. There was no one else left.

What Color is Today?

A.W. Lowery

In Irish, Neven means holy. However, nothing feels holy in a life that is slowly becoming undone… a life that is slowly becoming undone.

Neven has a rare form of Alzheimer's, which started to show on his 18th birthday. People didn't believe it. I mean how could they; memory loss is supposed to be an old person's problem. His attempts at explaining the mental lapses to others are often dismissed with rebuttals of him being a liar and faking it. I mean Alzheimer's is an old person's disease!

To hold onto the memories he holds most precious, Neven repeats them aloud until he can note and store them in his binders. A different binder for each day of the week. The binders read:

"Monday is RED,

Tuesday is ORANGE,

Wednesday is YELLOW,

Thursday is GREEN,

Friday is BLUE,

Saturday is INDIGO

and Sunday is VIOLET."

(Repeat)

"Monday is RED,

Tuesday is ORANGE,

Wednesday is YELLOW,

Thursday is GREEN,

Friday is BLUE,

Saturday is INDIGO

and Sunday is VIOLET."

Today is a GREEN Day, that means he needs to mow the grass, rake the leaves and trim the hedges for his parents. You see, he knows that, because it's in his green binder. Grass is green, the hedges are green, so the binder must be green and it must be a GREEN day.

Neven wakes up early and goes into the garage to fuel up the lawnmower. "It's supposed to be a busy day, might as well get a jump on it," he murmurs to himself. Neven presses the release to open the garage door, but he sees nothing but WHITE. A snowstorm quietly blew through the town during the night and painted it WHITE. He looks up to the sky and the storm's overcast is still sleeping on top of the town. He walks a few feet out from the house and turns around to see the house, the trees, the hedge all covered. It's like a painting covered up to create a new blank canvas.

Neven starts trembling with discomfort. "There must be some mistake, isn't today supposed to be a GREEN day? But there is no GREEN!"

"What is Today?"

why are you crying in an adult pottery class

Susie Rodriguez

why are you crying in this adult pottery class?

what the fuck is wrong with you? the clay beat against my hands and through my fingers. i couldn't even see the broken pile of the body that i was turning anymore. its crumbled skull lay like a mountain that had collapsed in on itself, and its hands seemed to reach out and then give up like the mouth of a river that was slowly eating away at itself, the banks, the ground only held together now by the ancient, gnarled grasp of the willow roots clinging. it was unrecognizable.

unrecognizable, yet she knew what it had been. she could still recognize the hollowed beauty, the melted beauty. her feet still turned the table. her mouth still held hope. her eyes stung.

it had been the most beautiful thing she had ever seen in her life, the most incredible creation she had ever built, and she had built it. she had. the hours to days to months to years to sunsets and sunsets and sunsets and sunsets it had taken to get to this place. to sculpt this being into the air. god, her eyes burned. how could she give up on it now? now that the other shoe had dropped, shattering across the hard earth like her father's antique crystal panes which she had fashioned into a gift, a gift shattering. her eyes burned and her feet sprinted. and. and how could she just give up on it? on everything she had been through with this clay body. her clay body.

she couldn't let it go. she held on to it. but how could she keep going? how could she hold on to something that wasn't meant to be held together? her body had morphed in its rebuilding and rebuilding. time after time after time after time. because this wasn't the first time her body had broken. not at all. it had fallen apart more times now, she thought as her fingernails plunged in again, than it had come together. but she couldn't let go of its beginning, the sublimeness of the idea that had pulsed through her heart and soul and mind when she first discovered it, when she first thought its possibility into being those years ago. how had it been so many years ? god, the blaze of inspiration that overtook her made her pump her foot again in panic of losing the fire! what if i never create such beauty again? what if i lose my love of creation all together without this! her breathing caught in her throat, and her sobs broke then, gasping at the edge of a waterfall she had been swimming against, like losing everything she had to save it she screamed. no one looked up. her classmates didn't even bat an eye anymore. they had heard these cries too many times to understand anymore. they couldn't understand anymore. they couldn't help. she hid her face in her clay covered arm and cried. she just cried. she just cried.

but her eyes burned and then her hands lost grip and her feet slowed their pumping, and for just a moment she felt relief. she felt her struggle dissipate. her heart rest.

build something new, her teacher said. build something new.

build something for yourself, her teacher said, and she laid her hand on her shoulder. you can't fix this body. you can't save it. she said, you can't fix it anymore. there's nothing left to do. her effort was so beautiful. but. enough. you already did it all. she looked up from her darkness and her teacher was still there. her classmates were still there, even though she had moved seats away from them in her effort to keep working. distance growing over the years, but still no more than a few steps away if she chose to.

build something new her hands said to her. build something new her feet danced to her. build something new her eyes cooled to her. build something new her heart sang.

deeply and fully and wholly. and like the sky. oh god, i remember the sky.

abruptly, she took her foot off the pedal.

her hands still covered in mud, lifting from the body. she breathed in. she breathed out again. she wiped her tears from her eyes with her wrist. enough. enough now.

she said, that's enough.

83

SECRET RECIPE FOR: CONNECTIONS

While we may have all come from the same college, we lead completely different lives. Ali tells us a bit about how that's possible...

Well. Virgil said write about friendship

and I'm writing this shit instead

(this is what you have signed up for, Virgil,

the power has gone to my head).

So, friendship.

Are we friends because fate locked us all in together?

(and fate in this instance of course has a name)

But then fate also took a year off, that one time,

So, M cannot be the one that we blame.

No, I think we have taken it slow with each other.

I think that together we've grown.

The point of a workshop is not to be stagnant

and the soft heart of art is to make yourself known.

Even faceless enigmas are still OUR enigma (cough A.W. cough)

and you're still one of us even if you don't show (this one's you, Sam).

And we pray that poor Ketan reaches his destination

(does anyone else think he's stuck on the road?).

Writing is just putting words down on paper

and reading is getting to watch them unfurl.

So here I have written the names of my friends

just to put them out into the world.

We're a group of distractable miscreants (hi Susie!)

but distractions can lead us down brilliant new roads

and whenever it's time to crawl back to our writing

there's Maeghan to lead us all home.

It is one thing to dance among writers,

it is then quite another to keep them for good.

We have built something lovely together

and I think we all cherish it (just as we should).

There are some who say writing is lonely

but I've learned you don't have to be only alone.

Sometimes friendship is sitting and writing together

for fifteen (five more) minutes (five more) over the phone.

So, Virgil asked me to write this part

and that's why it wasn't on time (sorry Virgil!).

But Virgil asked me to write this part

and that's why it's (mostly) in rhyme. ♡

BUTTER PECAN

A refined and mature flavor. These stories are pensive, multifaceted, reverent, or melancholy. An earthy, grounding taste for your day.

3 Ways to Break a Curse

Susie Rodriguez

If you find yourself being followed, consumed, or gnarled by a dark misfortune...Don't fret. Simply, try out one or more of these natural, healing contortions:

1. Gather the hair of a lover, preferably unbeknownst, and scatter the passion-filled scraps about the sleeping quarters upon the bright height of the next Full Moon. Fall asleep within the silver puddles of the lover's locks intermingled with the sultry pools of Moonlight. Think of tender thoughts. Dream of lavender. Upon first light, regather each strand to return to owner along with one's own bundle of curling tresses. Be sure to save 3-5 of the best threads to blow across the morning air, still dew-filled, still chilled from the night's absolution. (Best for aliments of the heart, feet, and lower back).
2. Locate the nearest moonlit lagoon, and on a night when there *IS* no moon, write your intentions, whatever they may be, on a local leaf—works best if this foliole has come to you falling from the sky, a caught autumn leaf plucked from midair. On a stone write your woes. Tether them together with a string of twine and swim to the center with a sharp knife in one hand, or a pair of sewing shears. All in one motion, take a gallant breath, release the contraption, and follow its sinking.

   BEFORE IT DISAPPEARS, you must cut the cord.

       You must.

   ¡CORTA EL VÍNCULO!

       SNAP!

All at once the stone shall sink into the depths of the black gloom, carrying with it your malediction, your suffering, and your calamity, and allowing for your intentions, your power, to rise again to the surface. Leave the leaf in the loch. Thank the water. Walk home barefoot.

3. Speak to the curse, ask it to be kinder.

An Analysis of the Enigmatic Homo Sapien

M Sweezy

On a dying rock in the Backbone of Night, homo sapiens, commonly known as Humans, roam a pathway. With their young nearby, the humans enjoy a relaxing time in the sunshine before returning to the dizzying and never-ending work they have created for themselves.

On a bench we find a young human alone. Still several years from maturation, the young human strays from the comfort of her parents. Though she looks cute, she will grow up to be one of the deadliest predators in the galaxy. For now, the young human tries desperately to understand her role amongst her peers. If she fails, the results would be catastrophic.

Unaccustomed to the newly discovered weight within her own head, the little one finds herself lost. She nibbles softly at a sandwich prepared for by her parents. The parents will do everything they can to help their young into maturation. But, predators though they are, life is kind to no being, not even them.

Watch as the young one attempts to join the others. She will first venture communication with the alpha of the pack. A reference to a book which the alpha has not read. Following the alphas lead, the rest of the group laughs and turns away from the brave and lonely human. Though the attempt has failed, the young one doesn't let the others smell her fear. She returns to the safety of her bench, and resumes eating her sandwich.

Notice the rose creeping into her cheeks, the tear she will hide beneath her long mane. She has learned this from her mother, a method of survival. The sandwich now lays untouched next to her on the bench.

Amazingly, the young human will try again with a different pack. This time, the young one has learned from her mistake. Waiting for the alpha to acknowledge her, the young human holds her breath. This could be a moment of life and death. Another failure. Should this continue, the young one could be alone until death.

The bench has been taken over by a young mating couple, so the young one must pivot. She finds a softened space beneath a tree. Worn from the dangerous attempts she has weathered today, the young human lays herself on the ground. This time, no tears come. She has adopted the look of the alpha on her face, a face that her mother will have used for hunting and protecting her young.

Tired and rejected as she may be, the young human relaxes into enjoyment of the wind tickling the leaves of the tree. Tomorrow she will try again. But for today, the wonders of her rock will be enough.

Autumn Heart

Ketan Pandya

Autumn leaves shimmer,
crimson and golden,
crisped in autumn's cold embrace.
Though the weather grows cooler,
the colors reveal fall's warmth.

Autumn, a showcase,
stunning vistas abound,
a treat for all to see.
For those who love nature, like her,
it's the best nature can be.

Autumn is balanced,
cool weather, warm hearths,
comfortably fair.
Her nature is much the same,
friendly but always honest.

Autumn's atmosphere,
perfect soil for stories,
perfect for dreamers.
A dreamer in her own worlds,
a writer bringing them life.

Autumn, a guidepost,
a sign of what was, what will be,
to all those watching.
Never letting her friends forget
their worth, what they can achieve.

Horizon Composition

Ketan Pandya

She sits where the sky and the sea meet,

book in hand she reads quietly.

A warm breeze fills the air.

Observance completed,

practicing her craft,

she writes her own

compelling,

charming,

story.

How Sweet and Fitting

Samuel James

How sweet and fitting were for I

To have a cause for which to die.

Would that I–unto the breach;

Would that I–onto the beach;

Blade against a blade, or fire

Returning fire–following choirs

Who plunge and gutter, choke, and drown,

And yearn to sigh beneath the ground:

How sweet and fitting life could be

Were death not what was asked of me.

Invalid Ticket

A.W. Lowery

(Horn Sound)

"All aboard!"

Two-by-two, the passengers moved in a slow funeral procession along the pier. They were all noticeably wearing their 'Sunday Best' and moving at an uneasy pace.

"Pull up the anchor, and prepare to unhitch the mooring lines." (Background dialog)

As they approach the vessel, Charon, or CAPTAIN as he's known by his subordinates, stands in front of his makeshift podium and checks for their name in his ledge before extending his index finger and commanding.

"That's 2 silver pieces each for thee lot of ya. I reckon I'll even be accept'n silver teeth, if that's all ya got… hahaha!"

The passengers reach and pull from their eyes, 2 coins. Dropping the treasure into the palm of Charon's open hand, the poor souls continue their march up the ramp, and are swallowed by the encompassing darkness of the ferry boat's deck.

Charon takes a momentary pause to revel in all the wealth that he is accumulating.

"Rich, rich, rich… what will I buy with all my…"

"Captain, we are at capacity for this trip. What are your orders?" (Interruption)

Charon glares back at his helmsman.

"Grr… There should only be one more, tell them I said make room!"

"Captain says, Clear the deck for one more." (Helmsman)

"Clear the deck!" (Echoing background dialog)

Turning his attention back toward the podium, he looks ahead only to see no one. If not for their voice, more delicate than that of a mouse, he would not have thought to avert his gaze downward.

It is a small child. A little girl wearing a tattered, green Easter dress with yellow berets adorning her hair. She's maybe 5 or 6 years of age.

"That's 2 silver pieces for thee lot of ya. Hurry brat, you're wasting me time and costing me money."

As he looks at her, he notices her eyes were not filled with silver, nor anything other than the jade irises that had always been.

The girl pulls a crumbled slip of paper out of her pocket and presents it to him. It's a recent ticket from a circus.

Confused, Charon scans the ticket before staring back at the girl. He then grabs her by the collar and lifts her up so she's at eye level with him. Her eyes start to well up, but she does not cry. She's not afraid.

In a gruff tone he declares, "You should not be here."

Charon carefully releases the girl before falling to his knees to let out a sob.

"Go child, this journey is not for you. And take this."

Charon slides the girl the satchel for which he was storing his silver. Before shooing her away.

"Buy a new heading! One that will take you back... back home."

As she runs away, Charon turns towards the ship.

"All aboard, and over the River Styx!"

Lines on a Friend's Birthday

Samuel James

Be merry, friend, be gold and gay.
Is that what I'm supposed to say?
Colder grows the soul today.

Yes, when I hear a friend is older,
I can't help but shudder, colder.
Colder grows the soul today.

Be young, be young forever, please,
Resist the hour and hours, for me.
Or some years soon, my soul will freeze.

Take no command from celestial arcs:
Blind the night, ignore the larks.
My soul is growing cold and dark.

So won't you be a friend today.

Your birthday? Skip it—Say, "Go away!"

I'm scared my soul is old today.

No More Bad Hair Days

A.W. Lowery

Sitting on the stool, kicking my feet back and forth, I watch the barber drape his cape around my father's shoulders like a superhero as he remains seated in the red padded chair. As the barber pumps a pedal, the chair slowly elevates, levitating him above the floor.

(Barber)

So how far are we taking it down to? A 3, 2...

(Dad)

Make it a -1 and hold the onions. Also, my wife loves it when I sport the Mr. Clean look, so 86 the beard as well.

(Barber)

...Right ...Too bad you don't have the dashing good looks to match

In no time, he flies off the chair a new man, and fishes $20 out of his pocket.

(Barber)

What, you didn't have anything bigger? Forget it man, use that money for a decent hat. You look dead tired, perhaps find one that can cover that ugly mug of yours.

We cross the street and arrive at the hospital. As we enter my mother's room, I run to her bedside and give her a hug. My parents exchange glances with each other.

(Mom)

Damn, I wish you would have saved some of that hair for me, I'm all out.

Pinning

Susie Rodriguez

She was trying to remember the steps. Opening the case which held it, the fragile small wings, the eyes which were still bright red despite the time. Despite the freezing. She had stored it in a small plastic bag, separate from all the others that she had collected during that time when she was still living with her dad back at home, her heart still so unsettled even though the air smelled like a waterfall of green summer branches and her trees kept her safe in the isolated haven of her backyard. They had come in swarms, late in spring, last spring—before she left. Swarming and loud and glorious.

It had only been a year since she had returned, but it seemed so long ago now, she thought, as she began to delicately unwrap the creature, her cicada friend. She felt scared. She didn't know how to touch her. Her hands stopped.

Again, she tried to remember the steps.

It was hard to miss those days of comforting sadness, the sun lush and solitary, and the trees which sang. And she didn't miss it, no, but she wished it could have been different.

"Hey dad?" She called across the house to her father, who was opening and closing doors as he went from back porch to front porch carrying nails. "Dad? Do you know if we have any gloves?"

She placed the thawing cicada back down on the old foam pinning board that had been on the top shelf of the closet for the past two years. Everything was untouched, unchanged, preserved.

"What?!" Her dad yelled back from between porches.

"Gloves!!!"

"Loafs??!"

"No! Gloves! Like disposable rubber gloves!"

"Disposable rugs?! What?"

"Disposable gloves!! I know we had some somewhere! Have you seen any? I think we have those black and orange ones, remember?"

She looked down at the cicada which was still where it had just been, half unshrouded. Well, I don't need gloves. But step one, she knew was gloves. That was always step one. But it's been so long now since she had developed these steps, designing her own methods and composing, as she did, her own rhythm. Maybe she had grown out of her fear. She began again, cautious and deliberate, to lift the bag holding the cicada, but her hands, they (froze) stopped her. She didn't know how to touch her. She couldn't bring herself to. The fear trembled in the tips of her fingers. And she went back to remembering the steps.

Step one: gloves.

"Dad!" She yelled out again, before sighing and moving to get up from the desk where she sat.

"I don't know about any gloves!!" Her dad was now in the front room digging through a drawer.

"Don't you remember the black and orange ones??"

She was thinking of the gloves she had gotten a year ago when she re-stalked, but maybe they had run out again.

"Or the blue ones?" she said. She had bought blue gloves at the very beginning of the pandemic from Harris Teeter. She had bought so many, there had to be some lying around somewhere, there were so many!

"You mean like rubber gloves like for cleaning under the sink!?"

"No, like the thin ones! That you throw away. There has to be some around here, somewhere! We had like thousands of them!"

"I'm sorry, baby! I don't see any gloves!" She could hear him loudly rummaging through more drawers.

It was strange, how feelings resurface so easily. She hadn't been able to hide her sadness from him, back then, though she had tried. And now that she was doing better, she only felt the guilt and the shame, the shame of it, more sharply. She could hear the familiar sounds of her father beginning to drop what he was doing to help her, so she yelled back," Don't worry!!! I'll find some! It's oki!"

"Maybe in the car?"

She began searching through drawers herself, starting in the kitchen, which only had miscellaneous drawers full of ridiculous items, items that became part of the drawers. She went to the bathroom next and then to the first aid kits. No gloves. She looked in her old bedroom, in her old backpack, no gloves. She walked back down to the desk where the cicadas lay.

Step one: Gloves.

But she didn't have any. She sat down again, contemplating her glovelessness. She could never handle the bugs when they were dead. She hated dead bugs, they somehow chilled her to the bone. Their lifelessness, it seemed. Because when they lived, she could touch them—she loved to touch them then! When their wings moved and their bodies weren't so solid, not stiff. Their brittleness stirred in her a childhood fear, maybe a fear of hurting something, like having something so precious in your hands, and trying to love it. To show it how much it means to the world, its beauty, to be close to it, but then crushing it, destroying it. Crushing it in the process.

Poor creature. She looked at the cicada's outstretched legs softening. She remembered the moment she died in her hands as she tried to save her. The leaves and lightly soaked paper towels she tried to recoup her with. The tears she remembers. She couldn't be saved, back then, but now– but now enough time had passed that, perhaps, her life could still be important. Maybe it was ok that she had died, because sometimes things need to die in order to give other things a chance to become. Like her–this cicada–who died after giving birth, after the frenzy of summer swarms. Enough time had passed, hiding in the freezer, and now she was ready to face her again. To give her a new home in herself. Like she had always promised her, and herself, that she would do. She promised her. She promised. But step one was gloves, and she couldn't find any. And the desperation began to rise in her throat—she doesn't deserve this ending— and there was no going back in the freezer. She really only had one shot to do her justice, and—

"Here. Gloves!"

Her dad's voice came in behind her and, all of a sudden, a single, crinkled blue glove fell on the desk in front of her.

"Be careful of the cic–" She startled.

"There! Glove!" Her dad turned to get back to the porches before.

"Wait!!" She said, picking up the glove. "Thank you!! Dad! Where did you find this!"

"The car!" Her dad yelled back, as the sound of the front door swinging shut followed him.

Step one: gloves.

Step two: pins.

Radio 1 to Ghostface

M Sweezy

"Come in, Ghostface. This is Radio 1. Do you copy? Over."

"10-9, this is Radio 1. Radio Check. Ghostface, do you copy? Over."

"Come in. This is Radio 1 proceeding with message. Confirming location of telescope positioning according to last coordinates communicated. Over."

"Broadcasting from 41 Troutman Lane, Perial, Wyoming. Second level, first door on the right. Bottom bunk. Over."

"10-5 to Alpha—let the record show Alpha related to Grandma Hester, benefactor of telescope belonging to Radio 1—Mom has relapsed into her recipe phase. Tonight's kill was meatloaf made entirely of tofu and dungbean. Radio 1 is considering a hunger strike. Over."

"10-6. Radio interference caused by air conditioning unit. Stand by. Over."

"Come in, this is Radio 1. Any updates on the question transmitted last night, October 12, at 22:20? Over."

"Radio 1 reiterating signals. Once for no, twice for yes. Over."

"You would hate the new Geometry teacher. Smells like bologna. It's a good thing you aren't here. Over."

"Disregard previous message. Over."

"Experiments on Algernon are progressing as planned. Hope to have Trick #3 completed by end of the week. Mom says I'm using too much cheese. I told her if I can make him roll over three times, we can make it into Guinness and make so much money I can pay for the cheese myself. Over."

"How is it going there? Over."

"Come in, Ghostface. This is Radio 1. Over."

"This is Radio 1, attempting Experiment number 231. Ghostface, do you copy? Over."

"This is Radio 1. Let the record show language established on October 22. Blink once for no, twice for yes. Over."

"Come in, Ghostface. Once for no, twice for yes. Over."

"10-9. 10-9! Eyes on target. Over."

"10-9. 10-9. Over."

"10-9. Radio interference by canine—get down, Maggie. Maggie! Ghostface, do you copy? Stand by. Over."

"10-9 10.9 Repeat message. Repe—"

"10-4, Ghostface. Loud and clear. Over."

"Let the records show two shooting stars entered the northwestern horizon at approximately 22:30. Radio 1 has made contact with Ghostface. Over."

"I miss you, too. Over."

"What's heaven like?"

"I think I'll be with you soon."

"I love you. Over."

Skater Boy

Virgil Thornton II

He balanced on his skateboard, hands in his pockets, a *Bleach* manga in the crook of his arm. Spring air coursed across his face, ruffling his hoodie, clinking the chains and trinkets on his backpack. He kicked, pushed, kicked, pushed, coasted down the hill, a lazy wave to the Jones kids in the cul-de-sac playing basketball. Ms. Brown flashed a smile at him as she jogged by.

He curved into the dark corner of gravel and drooping tree branches at the start of the forest trail. This part of the neighborhood was always empty around this time, and now was no exception. He scraped to a stop, flipping his skateboard up into his hands, then trotted to the usual spot. Sure enough, he could see the beady eyes of the neighborhood stray looking up at him.

He sat next to her, and unlike the first few times, she didn't run. She stared at him softly. He produced a can of cat food (and a can opener, the first time was quite embarrassing), then put dinner in front of her. She began to eat, and he cracked open his manga. One day when he had more money, he hoped to buy the whole series so he could read it any time he wanted. He loved the way the sunset painted the pages rose-gold. For a moment, he sat and enjoyed the peace and quiet. Then, he felt something brush against his leg. Did something fall off his lap? No, she was nuzzled up against him!

He paused, stunned. This had never happened before. He figured the cat always stuck around just for the food. Was she a fan of *him*, too? Gentle and testing, he reached out to her back. Embarrassing as it was, he'd never actually pet a cat, or any animal, before. He imitated what he'd seen people doing in shows and commercials, gliding his palm across the cool fur of her back. No scratches, no hissing, not even a glance up. It was like they had always been buddies. He did it a few more times, then went back to his manga.

He read, she watched the woods, and the two of them chilled out there until the sun finally set. Then, he bade her farewell and skated back home under the glow of the streetlights.

****

Kai knew the *ka-koot-ka-koot-ka-koot* from anywhere. Their mood dropped, as did their stomach, and before they could turn around fully, they were shoved hard. Books fell out of their hands, the ground rushed against them, and a sharp pain bloomed to life as they skinned their knee. Darius kicked his skateboard into his hand.

"Watch your step. Pink-haired freak."

Kai forced down a surge of hatred and fear, biting their cheek and collecting their books. People always said that not engaging a bully took the wind out of his sails. Mindless trash. Everybody wanted to tell them how to deal with a bully, but all that advice never came from experience.

Before Kai could pick up their *Bleach* manga, Darius scooped it up, tossing the previous chapter at the kneeling student.

"You actually like this trash?"

Kai said nothing, wavering to their feet. He didn't push them again like he sometimes did in the past. Even standing, Darius was a half-head taller than them, leering with a threatening coldness in his expression.

"How much money you bring for lunch today?"

"It's none of your business."

Darius grunted and Kai felt fear prickle across their skin.

"Want me to bust the other knee? How 'bout it, then?"

Kai could feel tears burning in their bottom eyelids. They had to focus hard not to cry. They hated, *hated*, HATED Darius. Why couldn't he just leave them alone? They went to say something and Darius stepped forward, making them choke on their words.

"Hurry up, Pinkie."

Kai obliged. They simply weren't strong enough. The tears fell as they fished the bills out of their pocket. Darius didn't comment.

"W-why do you always ask me for money?" Kai's voice came out watery and shaky in the beginning, curdling with rage as they finished the sentence.

"Don't worry 'bout it."

"Fine," they huffed, face pounding red like their knee, "I don't mind donating to the poor."

They held out the bills as if holding up a middle finger. The glare Darius gave made their blood run cold. They could almost feel his punch coming. But when Darius swung, it was instead to snatch the bills.

"Say some wack shit like that again and imma pop you in ya mouth." He stuffed the bills in his hoodie pocket, "This ain't for me, Pepto. You stay in your lane and play nice, maybe I don't hit you next time."

Kai sneered, feeling emboldened, "What if I don't bring you money next week then? Huh?"

They were shoved hard, faster than they could react, and crumpled to the ground again. After another lingering glare, Darius turned and skated off towards school.

You Laugh, I Choke

Maeghan Klinker

We live in an age of humor

and the whole world is in on the joke--

Can't you hear?

Bulldozers tickle the forest floor

and the trees grip their sides and fall

laughing

without a sound.

Gas bubbles joyfully from a pipe

and bursts into hilarious flame

right there on the ocean

without a care,

and the calving shelves

of ice rumble

as the glaciers crack up

without even trying to

contain themselves.

The seals are laughing so hard

that they choke

on the plastic rings around their

necks, and a turtle

snorts milk

right through the straw

lodged in its nostril.

The fish swallow teasing

nurdles of plastic

left like wry fortunes

tucked into each

fortune cookie current

and repeat the joke

to the pelican that

takes them out for lunch.

The joke gets funnier

and funnier

each time they tell it

until the pelican

keels over right there

and dies from laughter

all tangled with the plastic

in its gut.

BUILD YOUR OWN WAFFLE

A collection of prompts and ingredients used throughout the year. Some of them might even be in your favorite dishes!

A character with the goal to:

- admit to their girlfriend that they are a shapeshifter without it getting awkward.
- be liked by everyone.
- become a writer on SNL and to win an Oscar eventually.
- become the best tattoo artist in the city.
- break up with their partner of 5 years, a partner that they truly and deeply love but the relationship is no longer working—has it ever worked?— and is causing more trauma than love.
- expand their recipe repertoire.
- find my sister's killer.
- keep an office plant alive.
- maim and destroy a person who they once loved (and possibly still do).
- make the perfect taco.
- master a basic water spell. [*page 10*]
- perfectly recreate an idolized red velvet cake recipe consumed in childhood. [*page 70*]
- purchase a shoe rack.
- sell the most Girl Scout cookies.
- touch grass.
- unleash the Sealed Shadow Arts in the middle of Town Square to show the world the true power of Darkness Ninjutsu.
- win a short story writing award of any kind.
- win the Great British bake-off.

A mysterious package from no one arrives, and the contents are destroyed....

Aliens [*pages 23, 27, 34, 90*]

Each year Oxford Languages names a Word of the Year that reflects the "ethos, mood, or preoccupations of the past twelve months" based on thorough analysis of statistics and data, but for the first time this year's choice was open to a public vote. More than 300,000 people cast their vote and the overwhelming winner is "goblin mode," a slang term defined as "a type of behavior which is unapologetically self-indulgent, lazy, slovenly, or greedy, typically in a way that rejects social norms or expectations." Write an essay about a time you have gone into "goblin mode." Was the period of unapologetic behavior necessary for you to recharge?

Everyone is giving someone else an object, a sound, and a personality trait.

- [*page 66 - brazier, hush of scissors cutting paper, gullible*]
- [*page 77 - a dirty paper towel, a joyful scream, all-consuming possessiveness*]
- [*page 80 - color-coded binder set, a steady lawnmower, compulsive liar*]
- [*page 106 - telescope, air handler/conditioner hum, nervous inability to stop talking*]

Goulash [*pages 12, 16*]

L'Enfant Plaza becomes empty and very eerie on weekends. Create a cast of characters and write a synopsis for a five-minute horror short film set at L'Enfant Plaza.

Step 1: take 5-10 minutes and think about 1 or 2 things that everyone in the workshop does particularly well in their writing.

Step 2: think about some element that you want to work on in your own writing. Consider how other writers you admire (in workshop or not) achieve those elements.

Take a classic story/genre (space opera, Romeo & Juliet, tragic hero, etc.,) and put it in the sociopolitical landscape of an elementary school.

Think of something you know how to do that involves a complex series of specific actions…If nothing comes to mind…look up a process…Write a scene, involving at least two people, in which this process is going on, either in the background of a conversation or as the locus of the action. Keep the description specific and concrete. [*pages 7, 61, 102*]

We are thinking about pacing. 1) write a scene 2) now rewrite it thinking about ways to slow the pace way down 3) now rewrite the scene and speed up the pacing. [*pages 59, 72*]

Write a curse breaking poem for M. [*page 88*]

Write a description of a setting, then swap and write a piece in someone else's setting. [*page 18*]

Write a letter from the perspective of an inanimate object in a busy city. Describe the sights, sounds, and emotions you witness every day as you observe the lives of people passing by. [*page 54*]

Write a piece about a trick or a treat!

Write a poem for a friend's birthday. [*pages 29, 92, 94, 95, 98*]

Write a poem that mixes dark humor with a serious subject matter. How does integrating humor help balance and enliven the voice in your poem? [*pages 100, 111*]

Write a poem that reflects your relationship to any ritual or superstition you believe in. [*page 30*]

Write a story about the Wild Hunt. [*pages 45, 49*]

Write a story that begins at the base of a tree. [*page 38*]

Write a sympathetic character... then make them the villain. [*pages 75, 108*]

Write about a death and a rebirth. [*pages 41, 52, 96*]

Write about a haunting. [*page 48*]

Write something autumnal!

You wake up one morning to find that everyone around you has vanished. There are no signs of struggle or explanation. Write a suspenseful story about your journey to uncover the truth and find other survivors.

MEET THE COOKS

The Wafflers Workshop consists of Virginia Tech alum writers in a variety of careers. They get together weekly to practice their passion.

A.W. Lowery

A.W. has an eye for film. Enigmatic on the outside, pensive on the inside. I would tell you about all of his brilliant movie ideas, but his team of elite lawyer-ninjas (and ninja-lawyers) would ensure I wouldn't survive the week.

Ali Miller

Ali is not crazy, but rather, she is a normal girl, just like you and me. If she could, I think she would curl up with the sea as a blanket and look at musicals projected across the stars for the rest of history. That, and tell you neat trivia facts.

Ketan Pandya

Ketan is a pragmatist. He sees the world from a logical, reasonable perspective, and thusly would end humanity in one swift button press if given the opportunity. Unless, of course, you were to offer him a pack of Oreos, in which case, our collective doom might be temporarily postponed.

M Sweezy

M is a pharmacist, not in profession, but because laughter is the best medicine and she's your gal for that. Think: cool rollerblader that would also give you cookies and lemonade and freshly-picked daisies just because. She's that but, like, ten times more fun.

Maeghan Klinker

Maeghan, the Tree Lord, is our venerable dictator. I am contractually obligated to say kind things about her, which is easy because she is awesome. With a magic wand, she would probably use her unchecked power to viciously mandate greener, more sustainable solutions for all.

Samuel James

Samuel dwells in the shadows, not ominously, but rather as a hobby. He stays silent most of the time, plucking the brilliant, writhing ideas from his head only when they are needed. The sauciest ones he will gladly pluck and fold into the pages of his writing.

Susie Rodriguez

Susie is a beautiful butterfly, both figuratively and literally. The blood red of her undying rage and the bright blue of her cheerful optimism combine to make a lovely, artistic purple. Everything she touches is alight with her breezy delightfulness.

Virgil Thornton II

Virgil is me, the guy who does the thing. He was born at a very young age and is an expert in trying not to slouch and making funny mouth sound effects. He hopes you will support him and his friends as they continue to make cool stuff.

For more, visit:
weirddisciple.com

Made in the USA
Columbia, SC
25 October 2024